THE COCONUT BOOK

by
Richard Maynard

D1349555

SOUVENIR PRESS

ISBN 0 285 62709 0

Photoset by Inforum, Ltd, Portsmouth
Printed and bound in
Great Britain by
Mackays of Chatham Ltd, Kent

CONTENTS

Prologue   9

The Coconut Book   21

Epilogue   169

PROLOGUE

This is the story of a man. That is a bald statement, but there is little more that I can add. He is a nameless and faceless man. Who he was and what he was are still unanswered questions, and the likelihood is that they will remain so. But a man is more, so very much more, than a name, and so much more than a face. Names, after all, are merely tools for identification within a society. They are given with love, perhaps, and care, and they carry woven in them the power of human sentiment, but in the cold analysis of record they are only words; written on paper, they are just printed letters that can convey nothing of the personality they identify. Faces, too, are often deceivers. Can a man be judged by warm brown eyes, by a kind or a trusting gaze? Are eyes honest? Are they really the windows of the mind? Oh, I am sure we shall continue to judge men and women by their eyes and the projection they display, for we all have an inbuilt faith in our own judgements; we have faith in faces, no matter how often that faith is proven unreliable. Is that unfair? Perhaps it is. Faces often do reflect the nature of the person behind them, yet, as often, they do not. Natures change, moods alter with great frequency, but faces remain much the same.

The man in this story must, of course, have had a name, as he must have had a face, but more importantly, he had a soul. He had a soul and a mind and they are laid out as his identity surely with greater accuracy than a mere name could give. His story is so candid that one cannot doubt that this is a man as he is, without any pretence, without the dishonesty of a social face, without the false statements of social converse, and without all the constraints of social responsibility. But I do still regret that I cannot give him a name.

We are setting out now to find him, this man who wrote the Coconut Book. The quest is hopeless – deep down I recognise that – for there are too few clues, and surely he must be dead. But we shall look, if only to satisfy Watson, although that motive by itself is too shallow and could not on its own warrant the effort. But I have my own commitment, and beyond that lies that strange implicit faith men have in luck, the faith that even the thousand-to-one chance will come off if one pursues it with enough purpose. I think that that is my most powerful imperative. There are 50 thousand dollars to spend. That was Watson's testament to his own faith. It was unexpected, but Watson's death was also unexpected. He was with me when I found the Coconut Book, a seemingly vigorous and active man. Four months later he was dead.

❖   ❖   ❖

We were passengers on the yacht *Galathea* then. It was not possible to tell that Watson was a man of some wealth, for he was as shabby and unpretentious as the rest of us. He was tall and thin, quite extraordinarily thin. His face was also long and thin, a lugubrious face with eyes that protruded anxiously. That was deceptive, for Watson was anything but an anxious person, although he must have been a sick man even then. He never revealed the fact and we never learned of it until later. The *Galathea* is what is known as a luxury yacht, about sixty feet long and fitted for passenger cruising, supposedly giving its clients 'the holiday of their dreams' sailing the waters of the South East Pacific and North Australian coast. Well, we enjoyed our holiday, so the claim, though exaggerated, does hold some element of truth. The weather remained unbelievably serene, so that one could almost consider it part of the whole package deal. My wife, Val, has ever since claimed credit for it, because it was entirely due to her persuasion that we took our holiday on the yacht.

Even if we had not found the Coconut Book the decision would not have been regretted. The food was excellent, although the wine was no more than ordinary; the entertainment consisted mainly of the idleness that I had hoped for, without sophistication or obnoxious group activities, yet with enough exhilaration at times to make the cruise memorable. There were uninhabited islands, although our exploration was confined almost exclusively to the immediate beach. There were coral reefs, and they were exciting and beautiful. And there was the fishing – although in fact I only went on three trips for, in spite of there being ample opportunity, a sort of lassitude had pervaded me, a delight in doing nothing, and fishing does require a certain degree of enthusiasm at a given moment.

Had it not been for Watson, it is probable that I would not have gone fishing at all, but Watson was a born organiser as well as a dedicated fisherman, and he had my wife's encouragement in his attempts to persuade me. He really was a driving force. He endeavoured to organise fishing trips almost every time we anchored. Fortunately the skipper managed to dissuade him on most occasions.

It is only the third and last fishing trip that matters in the context of this story. We were somewhere near Bougainville, I believe. Later the skipper gave me the exact bearing for it may turn out to be important, it is one of our few clues. At the time, location was the least of my concerns. It was a reasonably calm day, perhaps with more swell than we had been used to and some clouds, extraordinarily white clouds, occupying half the sky. I remember thinking how immense the sky seemed. There was plenty of time for such thoughts, for the fishing was desultory, and perhaps it was that meditation, that simple wisdom derived from lazy reflection on the smallness of man in the vastness of the sea, that stayed with me and affected my later contemplations. There were three of us in one of the *Galathea*'s dinghies: Watson and myself, and one crewman to handle the outboard motor and the steering. His name was Paddy. He was a small, brown, toothless character, wrinkled and withered like a puppet; I am sure he considered his mouth's main purpose was as a place to put a cigarette, for he smoked continuously and hardly spoke a word.

11

Watson caught a fish, if my memory serves me correctly. I had had two strikes and had lost them both, which had prompted me to reel in my line and sit leaning over the boat's side with my chin on my hands and my arms draped along the polished rim, watching the sea move and feeling quite content. It was not hot, but neither was it chilly, and the motion of the boat and the swell moving rhythmically beneath us was hypnotic. It was noon or thereabouts. Watson was standing in the bow directing Paddy with a pointing arm. I don't know what he was proposing to do or where he was proposing to go. Then I saw the dark object moving as the sea moved, some twenty yards away. 'What's that?' I said.

'What's what?'

'That!' I pointed to the object. We were quickly leaving it behind. Then I gave my one and only command on that boat: 'Slow down, Paddy.'

'It's only a coconut,' said Watson sourly, possibly upset at having his authority usurped.

'It's got something wrapped round it.'

'Okay, Paddy, let's pick it up,' Watson sighed. 'And then let's get on with our fishing.'

A minute later I had the coconut within the boat. What had been wrapped around it was a denim ribbon used to tie the two halves of the husk together. Even Watson's curiosity was aroused at this oddity. The ribbon itself was beyond any usefulness and it fell apart as we handled it, having been held together by the fibres of the husk. We threw the bits overboard, and only later did we consider this action with some regret because they might have afforded us another clue, such as how long the coconut had been in the water. Still, we did not consider it at the time, and in truth it is doubtful whether such scraps of decomposed material would really have told us anything. Yet the husk was still difficult to force apart, as it had been married together with great care and also with some sort of adhesive. Inside was the nut itself, as one would expect, but it was a rather unusual coconut. The shell had had a neat circle cut at one end, about two inches in diameter, and this segment had been cemented back into place with great accuracy.

'Smash it open!' cried Watson. Paddy puffed away without emotion as if he picked up such objects every day of the year.

'No, we'd better not. We ought to open it in the presence of witnesses.' I had visions of illicit drugs or jewels, or something equally romantic. 'I think we ought to go straight back, don't you?' Such is the power of curiosity that Watson immediately agreed. But my caution was really quite unwarranted. All that was within the coconut was a book.

The book had been torn in two down the spine, presumably so that it would fit through the hole in the coconut. It was a paperback novel entitled *The River of Doom*, by an author unknown to any of us, Lawrence Severn. But Mr Severn's words are of no consequence, for his novel was used only as the vehicle for another writer to record his own chronicle. That chronicle is the substance of this book. It is the story of a castaway, although we did not realise that at first glance.

Indeed, our first reaction was one of acute disappointment. The yacht's crew had become curious enough to crowd round us as we prepared to break open the nut with a steel spike. Watson was there, of course, and so was Val. The coconut broke open easily enough. The revelation of the shabby document within produced no comment. Not immediately. Someone did say: 'It's only a book.' There was that dreadful sense of anticlimax. The crew lost interest and began to move away. I picked up the two pieces of the rather tattered document. It was cheap paper, now weathered and grubby. Nothing romantic about it at all. I sat amid the debris of the coconut feeling something like a conjuror whose trick has just failed. Val asked: 'Is there a message in it? There seems to be a lot of writing there.'

'There's writing everywhere,' I said. 'It can't be an SOS, anyway, it's much too long for that.' There was writing done with a pencil between every single printed line of the novel and on every conceivable blank area of paper. I was trying to fit the two halves together and made no attempt to read anything just then. The front cover bore a lurid scene of an almost naked

13

woman of extraordinary endowments sprawled unconvincingly on a raft amongst ferns and on a somewhat turbulent river. There was the inevitable serpent writhing in the foliage above her head. The text, we were to discover, was as unlikely as the cover, although the lurid scene itself did not in fact occur.

'Oh, my God!' was Watson's expressive comment. He straightened up and went to lean over the rail of the yacht. I had the feeling that he rather resented giving up his fishing time for *The River of Doom*.

'Never mind, dear,' said Val. She sat beside me and leaned against my shoulder. It helped. I did feel a trifle empty and foolish. I opened the book. There was a dedication on the frontispiece. Right in the centre, surrounded by confused pencillings, were the printed words: 'To my sister Harriet.' I began to read the first few words written at the top of that page.

'Listen,' I said. I reread the words aloud. 'Shock is with me still. And fatigue, although the memory of that swim is submerged already. I take up this pencil and write . . .' I continued haltingly, for the writing was most difficult to decipher. At the rail, Watson turned round and listened attentively.

Val exclaimed: 'It's a castaway. It's a diary!'

'He must have survived for some time to have filled up this book,' I remarked.

There is little point in recording here the details of the rest of our sojourn on the *Galathea*. I fear I have already trespassed too far beyond the boundaries of relevance. But there is one other significant conversation that I held with the skipper a day or two after the discovery of the Coconut Book. The skipper was known familiarly as Skip, but his actual name was Denis. He was a very large man and thickset, so that one felt a little daunted in his presence. Unjustifiably, I hasten to add, for Denis was an extremely amiable character.

'Denis,' I asked him, 'where do you think the coconut could have come from?'

He shrugged. 'Anywhere between here and South America. There's not much in between, you know.' He cracked his knuckles. It was a habit that he had and one that I found very irritating.

'In this latitude, though?'

'Well, we're just south of the fifth parallel, but that doesn't mean much. I'll give you the exact position of where the coconut was picked up, if you like, but it could have been floating about for years, who knows how many years? It could have drifted north or south many times, over thousands of miles, under the power of the wind alone.'

'But surely it would have sunk if it had been in the water that long.'

'Oh no.' Crack went another knuckle. I winced. 'Coconuts will float almost forever. That's why so much of the South Pacific has them.'

'Are you saying there'd be little chance of finding this island?'

'Virtually none at all, I'd say. Look, there are hundreds of islands and atolls all over the South Pacific, many uncharted, and islets of the size you'd be looking for might number in the thousands.' Crack, crack. 'I'll tell you this, though: it would have to be to the east of here, certainly not west.'

'Thanks a million,' I said, and retreated from the knuckles.

＊　　＊　　＊

Islands are the foundations for dreams; they capture one's imagination, and, like all people, I fell under their spell. For a time. The Coconut Book has subdued my fascination for islands significantly. I suppose most of us have had our fantasies of an island paradise where one can opt out of the mainstream of living and slip into the tranquillity of an aloof existence, with or without a number of records. No doubt the famous stories about castaways that we read as children, *The Coral Island*, *The Swiss Family Robinson*, *Robinson Crusoe* – to name perhaps the most well known – have all contributed to our adult daydreams. The reality of such an existence rarely occurs to us. After all, the islands of fiction are well supplied

15

with the basics of living: fresh water and an abundance of tropical fruit, also animals both wild and domestic. The Swiss Family Robinson had a whole farmyard with which to commence their island life.

'I wouldn't want to live on an island,' Watson stated emphatically, 'even if it did have a whole farmyard. I'm afraid that I'm your complete city type.' He was a company director, we had discovered. 'Oh, I like getting out onto the sea occasionally, I like fishing and I like the wide open spaces, but in moderation, you know, and as and when I choose.' The time was some weeks after our holiday on the *Galathea* and Watson was having dinner with us.

'What if you had no choice?' asked Val.

'Like that fellow?' He meant the author of the Coconut Book. He shook his head. 'No, I wouldn't make it. I haven't the necessary attitude, you know. Besides, I can't swim, you see, not very well.' He helped himself to another slice of ham. Watson lived alone. He had had a wife who had died many years before, but he had no children. He was not a lonely man, however, for his affairs kept him well occupied, but he did seem to value our friendship. We enjoyed his company as well, and he had maintained a strong interest in the Coconut Book.

'I wonder what one would do,' mused my wife, passing Watson the salt. 'Do you think many people have been in such situations?'

I answered her. 'Probably, especially during the war. Denis told me that there are thousands of such islands in the South Pacific and I imagine that many a wartime pilot found himself stranded on an island.'

'Was ours a wartime casualty, do you think?' She stood up and placed my plate on top of her own to remove them. Watson was still eating.

'He never mentions the war,' I pointed out. 'Surely he would have done in such circumstances.'

'Oh, I don't know. He was really rather an odd man, wasn't he?' She did not wait for an answer but took our plates away to the kitchen.

16

'Why do you say that?'

'Well, all that weird philosophising. Doesn't seem normal, does it?'

'Navel gazing, I'd call it,' muttered Watson through his ham.

'Come now, that's a bit unfair,' I remonstrated. 'Put yourself in his place. Wouldn't you have spent a lot of time simply meditating? He didn't have much else to do, you know. So he was obsessed with the concepts of survival and freedom and of his soul. Wouldn't you be? All right, we can't always agree with his propositions, but he strikes me as being anything but rather odd, even at the end.'

'Calm down, there's no need to get upset,' said Val. She had come back into the room and she put a hand on my shoulder. She was right, I *was* a bit upset. I felt a need to defend him. I had become immersed in the deciphering of the chronicle and perhaps too immersed in his personality.

'Val, darling, that was a beautiful dinner.' Watson patted his stomach. He was so thin that I almost expected to see a bulge there like a snake after a meal. He had told me once, quite without rancour, that his nickname as a youth had been 'Tiger', not for any fierceness of behaviour but for his likeness to a snake. He leaned across to me and uttered: 'What about the ghosts?'

'Yes, those ghosts puzzle me, too,' added Val. She was smiling at Watson in recognition of his compliment, but addressing her remarks to me. She has an amazing ability to communicate in two separate directions at once.

'Are they so difficult to understand?' I evaded a direct answer. At that time they puzzled me as well.

'You know, I'd like to set out to look for him,' Watson stated. 'He could still be alive. That is possible, you know.'

'Do you really think so?' asked Val.

'Well, it depends how long that coconut had been floating about in the Pacific Ocean. That denim ribbon was pretty rotten, but how long would it last under those conditions?'

'Besides, where would you start to look?' I put in.

'Well, let's see what we know. Fact one: it's an island completely on its own, out of sight of any other land.'

'Maybe not,' Val interrupted. 'You could argue against that.' She removed Watson's plate and went out of the room again without elaborating.

Watson smiled. 'All right,' he said. 'But to continue. We have the record of a lone man stranded on an island. How did he get there? We know that he swam there following the crashing of an aeroplane. The island is terribly small, but we do know exactly what its dimensions are.'

We are told it measures 'two hundred and thirty-two yards across its widest point as near as I can judge, and three hundred and four yards long'.

'It has no topography worthy of description,' Watson continued, 'just a clump of coconut trees and no fauna.'

'There were turtles and seabirds,' I said.

He glared at me, his protuberant eyes severe beneath his almost hairless brows. As a company director, he did not like being corrected. 'I was coming to that,' he said. 'Fact two: it's somewhere in the South Pacific east of Bougainville. We know the direction of the currents in that part of the ocean and we know the prevailing winds. It isn't much, I agree, but it's something to go on.'

'You sound as if you're serious about looking for him,' I remarked.

He shrugged. 'Not really. I'd just like to, that's all. Can't resist a challenge, you know. My circumstances won't permit it, though. Not just now.' Even at that time we did not know he was a sick man.

Val came out of the kitchen carrying a Pavlova like the head of John the Baptist on a tray. 'What I'd like to know,' she said, depositing the grand dessert in the centre of the table, 'is what he looked like.'

'Doesn't that look absolutely yummy,' drooled the snake, and Val's question passed by without comment. Unfortunately we could not have answered her even had the Pavlova not distracted us. Not only do we have no face to describe, we do not know whether he was tall, short, slim, thickset, whether he was fair or dark; just that his hair was brown, which means very little. We do not know his age, though I suspect from his activeness that he was under forty. We don't know what he did for a living. We do know that he was English. We also know that he must have been reasonably educated, that he wore glasses, that he was an excellent swimmer and that he liked music. We know some other things, such as the names of some of his girlfriends. He does not at any time mention a wife or children of his own, but it would be presumptuous to draw conclusions from a lack of information. I have made many deductions of my own but it would be an impertinence to lay them before the reader. Those who read the Coconut Book will form their own opinions, and they are just as likely to be correct as mine, and equally likely to be incorrect.

We finished the Pavlova. I believe it was during its consumption that Watson made his commitment.

So now Val and I are on a yacht once more. Not the *Galathea*. This time it is a much more business-like craft, motorised, faster and larger than the *Galathea*. It is the *Sea Lord III*, and it does not stop for fishing trips or to explore coral reefs. I have its use for six months. Perhaps it will be time enough.

THE COCONUT BOOK

Shock is with me still. And fatigue, although the memory of that swim is submerged already. I take up this pencil and write. It is of no purpose but it is better than crying. I have cried too much; tears of pity, pity for me, grief, painful grief for Hugo. Why did you die? I don't understand. I don't understand at all. The writing is good. It helps me. Already I am calmer. I don't know what to do. What to eat. I shall want to eat in time, I suppose. Hunger isn't with me now.

※　　　※　　　※

I suppose I'm going to die. There appears to be no alternative, yet still I hope. I'm not too alarmed, even though I recognise my inevitable destiny. But that recognition is centred in my stomach, while my head with its foolish brain still turns without despair to the sea. To that endless, unvarying horizon, unbroken by hint of land, ship, smoke or even cloud. The vista is actually beautiful in its blueness and its serenity, but there is a monotony about it and I've become as indifferent to its beauty as it is indifferent to my fate. This is my third day here. It was Wednesday when the aeroplane crashed. Dear Hugo. Your loss hurts so much, the grief affects my thinking, and I need to think very clearly just now. If you were here we would survive. You were eminently a survivor. And yet you have not survived; only I, for a little while. Why do I record that it was Wednesday when it happened? How can it matter? Is it training that prompts me to register such trivia, or is it merely hope? Though for what I hope I really can't say. Ships will never come this way. There is nothing here to attract wandering

23

natives in canoes. There is nothing here at all, only seven trees, six coconut palms and one other that I don't recognise. They are huddled together over there. Apart from them, there is nothing here more than a few feet above sea level. And me.

So today is Friday. What can I eat? The coconuts will not sustain me and the supply is meagre. I drink from them for I have found no water. So death must come within days. I should be frantic, yet I am calm. Why am I so calm? I just feel unutterably bored, and I grieve for Hugo. There is nothing to do. This book and this pencil are my only relief. The sea below is clear. I can see fish. There are many fish, but without the means to catch them they can serve me no purpose but momentary distraction. And without water, how does it matter? Perhaps I should just swim back out to sea until I drown exhausted. Dear Hugo, shall I join you?

※   ※   ※

Now it is Sunday. I must conserve the coconuts, but I am so hungry. Yesterday I caught a crab. It was very small and I ate it raw. So far it has given me no ill effects. I see that there are shellfish in the shallow water. I have already tried to pry them loose with my fingers but they hold on most tenaciously. My tiny penknife would be useless and would certainly break. As it is my only cutting device, I can't risk it. Surely I can devise some method of freeing them.

Today is rather cold. The last three days have been warm but last night there was a noticeable drop in temperature. I didn't sleep, I was shivering so badly. My clothes are quite inadequate for such weather. If only I could light a fire. But I have no matches. I want to smoke. There are three cigarettes in my pocket and they are dry now, but there is no way to light them. In my wallet there is paper: a driving licence, several pound notes, a receipt from my dentist, half a letter which I kept for the address – and already I've forgotten who it was from – and my identity card. I also have my book, but I would be reluctant to burn that, not just yet, anyway. So I have paper, but no dry

24

wood. Still, there is this one tree with actual boughs; they are green but seem to be highly resinous, and I'm sure they'd burn. All I need is the means of ignition. How futile is modern man without his technology. But could any man, aborigine, bushman, light a fire in this barren place? I don't believe so. No man could light a fire here without matches.

My spirit is low. I still search the horizon, but the thought of death has taken hold of me now. I have no will to contrive or devise. I despair. I feel so lonely and so helpless. I am crying from emptiness and hunger. Oh, my God, I am so alone! Pity me. Oh, pity me!

It is still Sunday. The weather has turned very cold indeed. There is a wind that forces its way through my coat and shirt beneath, so that I feel clothing is of little use. How shall I survive the night? I have no shelter. There is not a single convenient rock that will provide cover. Perhaps I should bury myself in the sand. What point is there in writing this? Who will read it? In days I shall be dead and this insignificant novel will wither in the wind. I am small. I am futile. I am only a pitiful man.

❋   ❋   ❋

This is my seventh day. It rained on Monday and the pools of water are a blessing. I have been working on creating a bowl in a rock by wearing it down with another rock. If it rains again I shall have at least one small reservoir. In time I could create several of them. Evaporation will be a problem, but coconut leaves will help. But how pointless. The drive of any hope at all is weak in me. Why should I endeavour to prolong an inevitable end? Yet I am afraid to die. Now I do have the recognised, almost familiar apprehensiveness of death, where I believed that I was indifferent. I don't want to die here with no one to grieve, no one to know. I shrink from the thought of it, although it is more than just shrinking. Writing of it makes it sound like a calm, analysed emotion. Well, the writing does

25

help me control what is in fact a desperation, a physical desperation that causes me to pace around, to scan the flat horizon continually. I have already walked round the island twice today, both times hurriedly as if there were some result to be had from urgency. I know that it is foolishness, but my mind shares the desperation so that rational thought rarely occupies it. The thought occurs now, as I write, that even if I do see a ship I have no means of summoning it. I have no way of making a beacon and no high spot upon which to stand and wave my shirt.

I have eaten another two crabs and many small shellfish, each one but a gram of meat. Still, I am not yet weak. As I sit and write I dream of surviving. It is an impossibility, but that impossibility is fashioning itself into a hope, even now. I can feel the emotional processes within me as I allow my consciousness to stand aside and observe. It is a strange sort of detachment. But it is not sustainable; already it has passed. How stupid I am. I haven't touched the coconuts for two days, so the hope has been there, suppressed, but shadowing my thoughts since the rain.

Rubbing the rock occupies me. I do not yet see it as purpose, although it does have some objective. Do I recognise that it will be purpose, more than just a casual occupation with a small benefit? Depression still suffocates me. It is hard to whip up the germ of hope, but I see that the depression is not absolute.

Having written that, I was overtaken with laughter. I stood up and walked the beach laughing ridiculously. Am I going mad? So soon? Is that all the human mind can take? I won't accept it. What would Hugo do? He was more resourceful than I. He would do something. I must think about that, but what is there to do? What can I think about?

The beach is white, very white in the brightness of the sun and silver at night. It is made up of very tiny pieces of shell. I wonder at the countless millions of creatures it has taken to make that beach. It shelves very gradually on all sides of the island into the sea, but soon after entry into the water it seems to take a steeper gradient. There are reefs not far out, clearly

26

seen in the calm periods of the sea, and there are many of those. Most days are calm. The rocks of the island are older, I suppose; that would seem irrefutable. They are quite soft as rocks go, but as they aren't limestone, this island cannot be a decomposed coral reef; so one must assume its origin is volcanic, possibly the last vestige of a volcano rim, or perhaps not the last vestige. Are there other, similar islands in the vicinity? There are certainly none within range of my vision. But it's a flat place. It is far removed from a tropical paradise. There is no lagoon here, no native girl with flowers in her hair. Just seven trees and emptiness. Not even a cave for shelter. It must be the most abject place on the face of this earth. It is abominable.

✻   ✻   ✻

Another day. I realise now there are some things that I can do. I must do. The situation is beyond all probabilities, but there could be miracles of circumstance. Rescue cannot be ruled out entirely. I will believe in it. So plan to survive, for months, perhaps. Years can't be contemplated, for that thought already weakens my resolve.

These are my resources. These are my clothes; no shoes; for I kicked them off in the sea, but socks still, over there where I discarded them on the first day; thick woollen socks. I can't really envisage any value in them. I have trousers, strong denim and quite new; they should last me for some time. A leather belt; underpants, of course, and a singlet; a denim shirt with breast pockets. And there is my jacket which I tried frantically to remove in the ocean, but it was buttoned at the wrists and I was unable to undo the fastenings in the panic of my swim. It is made of heavy cotton and has four pockets and a row of buttons down the front. In retrospect it was fortunate that I didn't manage to discard it, for its pockets contained this book and two pencils, and also my glasses which I tucked into one of the pockets before scrambling from the aircraft. No other items of attire. In other pockets I had my wallet, a penknife only two inches long folded up, designed for no more than sharpening pencils or cleaning fingernails – it may turn out to be a most useful tool. I have a handkerchief and seven coins amounting to four and sevenpence, also the key to my room. Nothing else apart from my wristwatch. It is still going, ticking away the meaningless hours. It is undoubtedly the most futile possession of all. But thank God for the pencils. They are my vital crutch to sanity. I must be careful to conserve them, to keep the exposed lead short. I can afford infinite care. There is much time.

What can I recall of recommended survival technique? I have read something of this at some time, with never a thought that it would ever be necessary for me to adopt it. Let me think. First, establish one's resources; well, I've done that. Then establish one's priorities. They are certainly basic enough: water, food and shelter. There are other needs, too – mental occupation, exercise, company – but the priorities must be the first three. So, item one, water: I'll have to rely entirely upon rain and coconuts. It is very overcast today; it could easily rain again before nightfall. I must concentrate on deepening my rock basin and making other entrapment areas; if I have to depend upon the weather it will be vital to have as many reservoirs as possible. Item two, food: there are crabs, shellfish and the possibility of real fish if I can devise a means of catching them. Consider the fishing. Can I make a fish hook? What to use for a line? Will the crabs be adequate bait? They should be, but can I catch enough of them? I wonder if they are more active at night. I must examine the shore line progressively on moonlit nights. Observation must be the key to survival. Observation and intellect. But I am hungry. I am exceedingly hungry. Item three, shelter: there is a cleft some eighteen inches wide, just above the waterline on the other side of the island, into which I can just squeeze, crouched over. Perhaps I can do something with that, extend it with loose rocks and roof it over with palm fronds. As it is, it will be most uncomfortable and can only be considered as temporary. I had better begin a more substantial edifice of rocks very soon, although I doubt if there will be enough portable ones for a proper hut. But making it will have benefits, both in occupation and exercise. There is no solution to the need for company.

Having put down my intentions, the need now is for the determination to act upon them, but this resolution is difficult to maintain. I am assailed by inertia – not laziness, for I never considered myself to be a lazy person, but a lack of enthusiasm; no, it is more than that: it is hopelessness, it is having no real belief in the value of action. It is a sort of giving up.

❖   ❖   ❖

It didn't rain. There is no more water. I can last today, then I must have a coconut. It means climbing a tree. So far I have not had to do that, for there have been fallen ones, but even fallen ones present the problem of husking. My technique is of the crudest kind: simply smashing the nut repeatedly against a rock until the husk is shredded. It is a most energetic process. I am sure there must be a simpler way. And how does one climb a coconut tree? It looks a singularly difficult enterprise. The bark of a coconut palm is very rough indeed and I balk at the idea of actually shinning over such a surface. But I suppose it has to be done.

This morning is cloudless and warm. I am grateful for that, for I swam in the shallows a short while ago and the sun feels pleasant on my nakedness. At last I have collected one of the shellfish that cling so forcefully. I noticed one on a small rock and was able to force the rock loose, whereas to free the shellfish would have been beyond me. I think it's an abalone, but my knowledge of such things is limited. It is roughly circular and this one has a circumference of about four inches, though it's not very thick. Still, once I free it from the rock it will be solid food, and there are literally hundreds of them in the water. If I can't free it I shall have to smash the shell, but I prefer not to, for the shell itself could be a form of tool. I shall replace the rock in the water in the hope the circumstance will occur again. I shall litter the sea bed with flat rocks.

I also noticed a lobster in deeper water but my vision was

quite inadequate to catch it. There are many fish, and they didn't seem in the least alarmed at my presence in the water. If only I had some goggles and a spear. A spear could be devised. I shall try spearing one without goggles. Today my hope is strong.

It is sensuous lying here in absolute nakedness and absolute privacy. The sun bathes me gently and I dream of women. Hunger has not diminished my virility. I recall Martine, thin, pale, chestless Martine, whom I loved and whose memory is a slice of pain. I remember her unbelievable, wonderful passion, and I abandon myself to dreams of her, dreams that are cameos of memory, recollections of the things we did in the many fused moments of togetherness.

Then I was fiercely lustful. And now I am alone. The sense of loneliness pervades me more totally than in all the days before. It has crushed the hope of the morning. I cry with pity for myself. My face is wet. I am here, naked and limp, just whimpering. What a soulless, miserable being. What an abject sample of withered humanity, spirit spilled on the sand. This is 'I', craven and defeated.

But I cannot whip myself into resolution by abuse. How long shall I sit here wallowing in this misery? There is no sign of rain; the sky is cloudless. I shall have to think of climbing a coconut tree. I know I can't do it. I shall die of thirst with a drink only thirty feet above me.

What purpose in eating the abalone?

It is night now. I am still naked and it is colder. Soon it will be time to dress. I must dress for dinner; in truth I must, for my dinner will be a coconut and I couldn't climb the tree naked. It is difficult to see now and writing these words is an effort, but I want to do it. It is my one contact with sanity. I ran up and down the seashore this evening, prancing and dancing in my nudity. It somewhat alarmed me. Even now, so soon after, I can't recall the motives that prompted so ridiculous an activity. It was an excess of freedom when I can't be free. This island is a cell. How long can a man retain sanity without human contact?

30

Even a prisoner has a warder; there is always some point during the day when the most restricted captive has a moment, however fleeting, of human contact. A moment to feel hate, perhaps, a moment to utter words, even if those words are of defiance, a moment to convey some sort of emotion, some communication with a fellow being. In this cell there is nothing, not one instant in the future to wait for.

I'm cold now. It's time to dress. I remember a landlady who insisted upon her tenants dressing for dinner.

'Dress for dinner, please,' uttered Mrs McGinty. She had a voice that sounded like tyres on a wet road. But she was a formidable woman. Even Hugo would balk at challenging her. He used to retreat with grace, however.

'But, Mrs McGinty, I'm not undressed,' he said. On this occasion we stood at the door to her dining room, sweaty and varnished with dust, incongruous in our riding shorts in the pseudo-elegance of 'McGinty Hall', as Hugo called our boarding house. The six other faces in the dining room watched us palely and unspeaking from the dark polished table with the white doily in the centre. They appeared to be dressed. I had a vision of tweed jackets and navy-blue blazers beyond the impregnability of Mrs McGinty's thick red arm across the doorway.

'In this house you will not get fed dressed like that,' intoned Mrs McGinty implacably.

Hugo bowed with dignity. He was always dignified. Probably only I could see mockery in it. 'Madam, for your food I would wear ermine robes,' he told her.

'A coat and trousers will do.' She may have sensed a hint of mockery after all.

'What's for dinner, Mrs Mac?' I put in. I wanted to make sure the effort was going to be worthwhile.

'Fish,' she said, if my memory is dependable.

I would give anything now for a plate of Mrs McGinty's fish, though on that occasion I believe we elected to forgo the pleasure. We probably had fish and chips out of a newspaper.

Now I'll eat the abalone.

The shellfish was extremely tough. I chewed through it mouthful by mouthful during the night. It was raw and salty, but not an unpleasant taste, and it hasn't made me sick. I am very sore this morning, though. Reaching a coconut was more of an ordeal than I had imagined; I must be weaker than I realise. My descent was too quick and uncontrolled, and I tore the skin of my inner thighs and my hands. Still, I have had a drink. I drank half of a coconut and saved the rest for later on today. The rock is back in the water, and I just lie and rest, feeling my thighs hurting, but not too distressed.

I saved the shell, there was no need to break it; out of the water it was possible to cut the mollusc free with my penknife blade. It might be feasible to use the shell itself as a lever to free others from the sea bottom. I feel so sore, though, that I'm not yet willing to swim. There are some wisps of cloud in the east and also a breeze today. Ridiculously, it stirs my hopes of rain. What day is it? I've already lost count, which is of no consequence in itself but it is a pointer to an undesirable relaxation of principle. I suppose that's inevitable. This journal must become my anchor to morale, I see that clearly. The pencils must be made to last.

The sun glints annoyingly on my spectacles and I see the simplicity of lighting a fire. I can only be amazed at my own stupidity in not thinking of it before; it really seems so obvious. But I must ration my paper meticulously; there isn't very much, even using the pound notes. Fuel, too, must be conserved, although I suppose the dry coconut husks will burn. I look forward now to a cigarette. A little fire immediately will be an extravagance, but it takes so little to light a cigarette. Yes, I might as well make the experiment now.

It was quite simple, really; just a matter of concentrating the sun's rays with a lens onto a piece of paper and I am smoking a cigarette. I'll smoke just half today. Amazing how that small act has raised my hopes. The ability to make fire has extended not only my capacity as a human being, but more importantly, my confidence. I have made my first technical advance, much as some remote ancestor directed his species on the path to the stars with that selfsame technical achievement, although admittedly he hadn't the benefit of a pair of spectacles. It gives me another resource. I have to use it frugally, but knowing I have it, I am a man. I am strong. Stiff and sore, but with new valour. I can challenge my world. It will not limit me.

I have swum and dived all afternoon and I am exhausted. But I have seventeen abalone at my feet, and I have unlocked a virtually inexhaustible larder. They aren't an easy crop to reap; the technique is to slip my empty shell under one and to lever on the instant. It is vital to be quick, and that is difficult without vision in the water. If one fails initially, they immediately lock themselves to the ocean rock and can't be moved. The empty shell snapped several times and is now beyond usefulness. Yet there are seventeen others here, and tonight I shall eat a full meal for the first time in this blasted place. I must pound them to make them tender, as my mother used to do with certain cuts of meat. I can't cook them, for there is nothing in which to hold them over a fire, but cooking is a refinement of secondary importance at this moment. I need more to drink, but I still have half a coconut and the clouds are looming large in the sky. If it rains soon I shall have all the needs of life. But company.

I observed that fish were very attracted to damaged abalone. If I had a line and a hook the mollusc would make good bait. The zip fastener on my trousers has a loop of metal as a finger-grip; surely I could convert that into a hook. What can I use for a line? If I unravelled my socks, would wool be strong enough? Somehow I doubt it. What else do I have? Impossible to unravel denim or cotton, but there must be something. I shall have to give that some thought. But just now I have plenty to eat, my spirits are high, consciously and deliberately high, knowing that despondency is lurking like a ghoul at a corpse.

It hasn't rained again. I am very thirsty. However, at the east end of the island there is a depression behind a barrier of rocks that fills with the tide, though somewhat behind it, and drains more slowly than the receding sea. It would appear that the rock is porous at some point and my hope is that the substance of the rock may have a filtering effect on the sea water, reducing the salt content. I am prompted to test the theory immediately.

I have now tasted the water in the soak and it is absolutely awful, but in truth it is far less salty than the sea itself. It is unpalatable but it will sustain life, I think. I shall drink as little of it as possible, but it is some comfort to know I need not die of thirst.

The three most dreadful aspects of my existence here are, firstly, the unrelievable loneliness, and that is the greatest weapon of any threatening insanity; and then the overwhelming boredom. What can one do on a few miserable square yards of empty beach? The hours are tedious beyond expression. This pitiful novel is my most precious possession. And, thirdly, the impossibility of any degree of comfort. This is total discomfort, unrelieved and relentless; sleeping on sand, sand in my clothes, in my hair, in my beard, in the very pores of my skin. Nowhere is there any softness, and there is only the sea to wash in. And now my beard is becoming almost unbearable. I always hated beards. It makes me itch under my jaw and at my neck, and repeated immersion in the sea causes salt to deposit in it. I feel like tearing it out. The penknife is useless as a razor. I can only wait for it to grow and perhaps improve. I can recall accounts of stranded travellers who shaved daily to preserve the essence of dignity. I admit that I find that a somewhat absurd proposition. I would shave daily if I could, but only to preserve a degree of personal comfort. I wonder what I look like. There are no mirrors here, no placid pools to provide reflection. I have already forgotten my face, the exact colour of my eyes. I can remember other faces so much more clearly than my own.

Martine I see with absolute clarity, and Hugo; Paul, too. And Monique – such an unlikely name for so large a woman – I loved you, too, Monique, for a little while, so fat and soft and wonderfully warm. I loved you naked, with your gross white breasts, forever soft, enveloping me in gentle passion. I remember your convulsions that came so quickly, like ripples but still gentle, and then the permeating softness of your gratitude. But that was so long ago. Why are you now vivid in my mind? There were others since, though not so many; vague faces now, lost names; moments that were then so utter and are now so meaningless, obliterated in the futility of the past. You I remember, though, Monique, your face and your flesh, because I loved you. For a time I loved you. Now I recognise that. Then you were only fat and somewhat comic, and I left you without regret. Regret now is sharp, but perhaps not too sharp, for long after you there was Martine. So different, and I loved her more. I knew the fullness of the emotion with her, and that regret is an ache.

I have drifted from my thoughts of comfort and beards, but it helps to write as I feel. This slim book is my company, keeping the loneliness from overwhelming my faltering hope. I don't read it, it is an absurd story, but just to be able to write my own pitiful words between the clear, sharp words of the print gives me the most vital factor in my tenuous grip on sanity. This meagre book is a treasure worth more than any that could have been buried by pirates somewhere on this worthless place. Sometimes the wonderful romances of boyhood do capture my thoughts, and I imagine a map drawn in blood – it wouldn't take much for there is very little to draw – with an 'X' marking the magical spot. But romance is something that can only be sustained for a very short time. The reality is too harsh.

Night time is better than day. The immensity of my loneliness contracts to the limits of my vision. Then I can't see the unchanging horizon that withers me even as the sun cannot do.

35

By day I am reduced to a mote in the unviolated expanse, but night time encloses me with its friendly darkness, so that I am large within it. I see that size is relative. I wonder why that concept has never occurred to me before. Distance makes me small. At night there is no distance. There is no other gauge. If I were the tallest man on Earth, or the smallest, here it would have no relevance.

Depression is settling about me. It is so hard to be hopeful. The sky is blue, continually and monotonously blue. I want it to rain and I hate blue. How long have I been here? Does it matter? What does matter? Is there one thing in the whole of this execrable existence that I can say, in all truth, matters in any way at all? Not even my survival. The world wouldn't miss me, would hardly notice my absence. Oh, a few people would wonder what had become of me, and one or two might cry if they knew of my demise, but apart from a few particulars in an archive it would not matter if I had never been, and there would be no other trace of my passage. This is the lethargy of thought that I find myself slipping into all the time, and without some stimulus it is difficult to combat. I suppose I can live here indefinitely, although the very idea is too horrible to contemplate. How long before thoughts of suicide can't be suppressed? How long before I elect to swim out into that vastness and peace? Shall I be insane at the time? Shall I be a laughing, cackling caricature? That image appals me far more than the idea of death. I would elect to swim first. They say that drowning is the most pleasant of deaths, although that surely can't be verified. There could be sharks. I wouldn't want to die from shark attack.

*   *   *

I miss noise. This is a silent place, even the sea is quiet. It has a sound, of course, but it has established itself as a hush on my senses and I don't hear it, although now I have opened my consciousness to it I hear it well, for there isn't a single other sound to intrude. There is no wind in the trees, not at this moment, not even the squawk of a seabird. I long for music, for a Mozart symphony, or the voice of Caruso shattering the cloying stillness of this meaningless plot. I shout. I often shout. But the sound of one's own voice is insufficient to satisfy the craving for noise. In one's normal environment there is always noise. Noise is a habit, a factor, almost an essential factor in one's existence, and although there are times when one curses an excess of it, and times when one feels blessed due to the lack of it, it's only in the total absence of the intermingling noises, the myriad sounds of living, that one realises the essentiality of it. One was born with sound, one was reared in the cradle with the reassurance of voices and lullabies, and one developed with speech and music, with song and laughter. Sound. Soundlessness is like a death, a vacuum of the senses, and I am lost in it. It is a great part of my despair.

There was a girl called Sally who once had a momentary place in my life. I think her name was Sally, but her importance to me was fleeting, and Sally may have been some other girl. I took her to a concert in the City Hall. I remember it was a wet evening and we queued for almost an hour in the open, close together under her umbrella, just touching and feeling a new and exciting consciousness of our closeness, lowering our heads to mutter and giggle in private foolishness. The rain dripped off the umbrella. A person behind, without one, tried to crib a piece of our shelter. In the thrill of our nascent intimacy we kept him out. We were selfconscious in the dawning of blood, but happy.

Later, in the dry, unstirring tension of the hall, we held hands and the music played. The music was superb. I don't recall the girl, but I readily recall the music. It was Rachmaninov. I also remember they didn't put out the lights, so I closed my eyes. It was sound that required darkness, needed no such distraction as the wet hair and dripping coats of the audience. There were a lot of eyes closed. I was in rapture. The girl placed her free hand over mine already holding her other one, and squeezed gently between our mutual knees, perhaps mistaking the cause of my joy, but possibly sharing the enchantment.

37

Sally, if indeed it was Sally, faded quickly from my life and my caring. Something must have splintered the fragile bonds of new emotion. The music, though, of that wet night in the City Hall embedded itself in my mind for all time.

This morning I sang. I sang 'You are my sunshine,' over and over again. It wasn't Rachmaninov, but it helped. With wind there will be sound in the trees. And there are birds; I've seen them in flight about the eastern end of the island, although I haven't noticed one land.

❖   ❖   ❖

I have devised a method of climbing the coconut trees which will not only save damage to my skin, but will provide me with some occupation. It has given me a small purpose. It involves making a series of pegs using the timber from the odd tree, and driving the pegs at intervals of about two feet into alternate sides of a trunk. A simple enough project, one would think, but with limited technical aids, not at all simple. I must first cut off a bough from the odd tree without a proper cutting tool and then divide it up into the required lengths and fashion points at the ends. This can be done with the penknife so long as I take great care, because the blade is held to the case with only a slim brass pin and vigorous whittling will almost certainly fracture it. Then it will be necessary to drive the pegs into the palms with a rock without too much shredding of the ends, and as I progress up the trunk this will have to be done from the rungs below. Still, I shall do it. Abalone shells will have to serve as my cutting edges, and there is the infinite resource of time to take as much care as is needed. There's certainly no hurry, and my penknife is easily kept sharp on this type of rock; it makes a fairly adequate whetstone. In the meantime I'll have to drink from the brackish pool as the tide makes it available; I'm becoming accustomed to its taste; it's more the tang of the rock and the slime of the pool than of saltiness, that makes it unpalatable. It doesn't seem to stimulate a further need of water as the sea is reputed to do.

There is a need to catch some more shellfish, because most of the others began to smell before I managed to eat them. It's clearly rather pointless catching so many at one time. Today, though, I feel just a little apprehensive of the water; it was thinking about sharks that alarmed me. I did dive a short while ago, but my fancies became too strong and I left the water with only two shellfish, two very small shellfish. Nevertheless, I shall dive again later.

Once again there are no clouds, yet the sky seems more intensely blue today, not the pale, pastel colours of previous days. That should be no reason to raise my spirits. I don't know that it does, or whether it is having some purpose that helps me. But it is true that I have a more positive attitude at this moment. I feel that my life cannot be allowed to dwindle away, that my substance will not become spineless dust in the wind. I shall live, and somehow I shall hope. And I'll indulge in another little fire and smoke the other half of my earlier cigarette.

Within the confines of my island, ambition contracts, hopes and plans become minuscule, intruding little into tomorrow. The decision to create a flame and light a cigarette is one of the major convulsions of mind. It is the momentous event of the day. Actually the tobacco tastes vile after being immersed in salt water and dried out, but I refuse to allow the mere sense of taste to diminish my pleasure. The tobacco releases dreams, recollections of leisure and friends, conversation and the mellowness of inaction when inaction was itself an ambition. Half a cigarette doesn't last long, even when drawn to the final shred with the aid of a splinter. Now boredom, that ever-present, engulfing problem of all active intelligence. It leads me to depression. I seem unable to avoid it.

I shall measure the island. There is a purpose. A purpose with no objective at all except the one of record. To do it accurately it will be necessary to practise a one yard pace. I am the only object on the island of a known length, so if I mark my height on the sand by lying prone I shall be able to determine an exact yard. I shall do it, I shall do it now. It is a very small project, but it will relieve boredom for a short time. As my ambitions are small, so must my projects be small.

Now it is done. The island measures two hundred and thirty-two yards across its widest point as near as I can judge, and three hundred and four yards long. Six thousand square yards of barren rock. It has crevices and cracks and a covering of the shelly sand, but other than a handful of loose stones, appears to be one homogeneous mass. There is some soil under the coconut trees, just the humus of their leaves and husks deposited thinly on the sand. It is enough to support the one other tree, but not to inspire it into any vigour. Without knowing its type, I would consider it a deformed, sad thing, struggling like myself to survive with the most frugal nourishment. Perhaps it is young yet, or perhaps it's just tired, worn out with the competition for water and sustenance against the more able palms. The coconuts are arrogant by comparison. Arrogant and strong. They belong.

This, then, is my home, my island, my cell.

✳   ✳   ✳

It has rained. I prayed for rain and now that it has come I hate it. I have sound now, and fresh water, but I also have cold. The rain comes with wind from which I cannot hide. Even being huddled in my niche in the rocks doesn't shield me, and it's so uncomfortable crouched up like a hedgehog that it isn't worth the meagre protection. It is probably better to remain exposed. I do have a plan, half formed in the sump of my brain, to build a hut of stones thatched with palm leaves, but I haven't developed it because I know there aren't enough rocks, or enough leaves. If I fetched rocks from the sea bed there might be enough, but that is a labour so strenuous I balk at commencing it; I would have to dive and swim upwards clutching the rock. Well, it could be done, but there is no point in starting a labour I haven't the drive to complete.

I can't even light a fire for now there is no sun. I shiver

and find this writing difficult, although the book is kept dry beneath my shirt. It would be hard to imagine a more wretched human being than myself. The rain has stopped now but the wind continues. There is not one single spot in this abject place where I can escape the damnable wind. It is a thing of spite, whirling and inconstant so that, even huddled against the trees, I cannot avoid it. The cold I could take, I would endure that, but the shivering is eroding me. I have considered burying myself in the sand but the wind would blast fragments in my face and I fear that would be a worse torment. I can only wait, shiver and wait.

The wind has brought some birds to the island. There are eleven of them, grey and black birds with prominent heads and bills. They are as big as seagulls and very noisy. I would guess they are a type of gull but I don't recognise them. They have settled on the northern end of the island and twice I have gone over with the thought of catching one, but inspiration eludes me. They simply fly out to sea at my approach and return with a certain degree of disdain to some other spot.

Three coconuts have fallen. That is some benefit from the wind, but it reduces my available stock by a quarter and those that are left are immature. Still, mercifully I am not dependent on them. Even today I could swim if necessary, though the sea is dark and angry. Fortunately the windfalls will sustain me until the weather improves. Already I am more hopeful. The writing is my solace, despite the wind plucking at the pages, despite the shivering wilting me and making the pencil hard to control. Still the writing is a solace.

*　　*　　*

The wind blows still, but less than yesterday. I have buried my legs in the sand and pulled a sock over my head, cutting a hole to expose my face. It is some comfort and the shivering has been subdued. Incredibly, I am assailed by lust. Does aloneness exaggerate one's lust? Or is it the seafood? Do those damned shellfish contain some element to agitate the hormones? I can't recall any point in my life, even during my young manhood, when the blood strode so forceful and arrogant in my veins. It demands release and the release is pathetic. It is humiliating. I shall do nothing about it now.

I am heartily sick of shellfish. They would be a delicacy in rarity, cooked in herbs and butter, but raw and as a staple they have become distasteful. There are crabs. At night, especially nights of a bright moon, they do scurry about on the fringes of the sea. But they are pitifully small. Even several are of little value to a hungry stomach. Neither are they nice, for I am unable to separate the shell too well and find myself constantly spitting bits out; and the meat isn't pleasant uncooked. I long for fish. There is a length of bough on the odd tree, one only, that could feasibly be fashioned into a spear. When the sun comes out again I shall try. The fish aren't afraid. It should be possible.

Oh, God! Now the rain has started once more.

✲   ✲   ✲

I used to suffer dreadfully from headcolds. Anything would start one: not changing out of damp clothes; a climatic change; even getting out of bed on a cold night. By that tendency I should now have a very bad one indeed, but there's no hint of one, not a sniffle, not a sneeze. I must count that as a definite benefit, for there aren't many. Perhaps the very seclusion of this place makes it sterile. I haven't even had a headache here, not yet, and I was a constant sufferer previously. But I would trade these benefits for company. I would gladly suffer the most atrocious headache for one hour with another human being. Mankind is indoctrinated with the words intended to ease the pain of emotional tragedy – so long as you have your health. Good health is beyond price. I accepted that as most people do; it would seem such a self-evident remark. Now I see it as false. A convict would trade health for freedom; a mother would trade health for her child's life; I would certainly trade mine for many things. Without my good health, my survival would be more uncertain. But I have it and care little about surviving. It is easy to write that, yet not to survive is a decision I couldn't make. How meaningless my ponderings are becoming. I must divert myself from such a train of thought.

The wind has stopped now. And the rain. It isn't cold but there is no sun. I'm naked and my clothes are spread in hope. Hope is the description of my life. It isn't a shining beacon, not a constant, consistent drive springing from a determined will. It is something that fluctuates within me all the time, it has to be stoked like a fire. It's like a fire in the wind; the slightest breeze will diminish it, but if I feed it the wind will make it blaze. Any blaze, though, is short-lived. On a night such as the one just past, alone in the emptiness of nowhere, chilled and shivering, hope is barely an ember, frosted over with the ash of defeat. But I can boost it now as the day warms up and with a promise of sun.

I have shaped my spear. The abalone shells serve well as cutting tools, sturdier than the penknife. And there lies my great technological advance, less than a yard long, with a slight arc from the centre to the tip; the middle is just a bit wavy and the whole thing more flexible than one would like. But I have made it. It is my thing. I have read that primitive peoples harden the points of their spears in fire, but this wood is so resinous I don't feel inclined to take that risk. In spite of its patent deficiencies, I admit to a certain pride in the spear. I am not a resourceful man by nature. Resourcefulness with me is a labour of mind and willpower. I see now that in my previous way of life I leaned on other people, though unknowingly; I have been supported by the strength and inspiration of just a few individuals in my society. And in analysis I see that that is how the majority of people exist, that the resourceful people are really very few, they are the steel of society which supports the flimsier fabric between, the fabric that moves and rocks and breaks up under the various stresses of trying to be. Hugo was of the steel kind, too friendly, too tolerant to be a leader of men, but one of those we less confident mortals turned to automatically, unconsciously, when decision was needed.

Hugo would have laughed at my spear, not in ridicule but in jest, a gentle jest that would have been almost praise. Dear Hugo, I miss you so much.

Remember the bike rides. Those long, random, purposeless trips through the gentled countryside. You were always ahead, the strong white muscles of your thighs flashing jubilantly, it seemed, below your shorts. I followed them, mesmerised by their lack of pause and the dedication of my own effort. You always led. We were young then and as green and joyful as the coppled woods. We were hopeful and free, so very hopeful and so very free, untroubled in the troubling world. There were country inns – we discovered so many – and girls and beer and laughter. W were full of joy, and we sang; we sang as we rode, we sang at the inns and our songs were chorales of jubilation. I remember only the joy. Surely there were bad moments. There were aching legs. An accident, too, I recall, although the details have not remained. And there were always the fractures of our young and willing hearts. But the memories of joy are stronger. They remain as the fiction of a better past. Gratefully, they remain.

There will be joy again. I *will* believe in that. But not the joy of youth, not the joys shared with Hugo. Never again with Hugo.

My spear is useless. Apart from the problem of vision in the water, there is also the slowness of my movements. It was pathetic, really. I doubt if I even frightened the fish, they glided away so effortlessly from the thrusting stick, but as they are never where my eyes tell me they are, it is probable they didn't see the spear as a threat. I have to consider the problems further. I have to treat them as a challenge to my ingenuity. Think productively. Keep dismay at bay. I must be positive. But the void in my stomach is despair. I feel it spreading and engulfing me. The challenge is too difficult. I can't stand the taste of those blasted shellfish. The thought of eating one again revolts me. I must catch a fish. For the sake of my sanity I must catch a fish.

Another technological effort. I feel no elation in it this time, no pride; it is ludicrous, and it took so long. I have cut the legs off my trousers and sliced them into long strips by spiralling the cut up the leg. It was a tedious job without a pair of scissors. I had to hold the cloth with my teeth and one hand while slicing with the penknife. My jaws ache and now I have no covering for my legs, but I do have a long ribbon which is tough and unlikely to part with the tugging of any reasonably sized fish. I have used the fingergrip of my zip fastener for a hook, removing it with a great expenditure of effort from the fly of what is left of my trousers, bending it over and over again till the pivot finally parted. It was easier in fact to fashion it into a hook, although I have strong reservations about its effectiveness; it has too little rigidity, and it is only held to the ribbon by being forced through it in two places. I can't think of any other way. So there is my fishing line. It doesn't inspire me with confidence. There is some comfort in the thought that, even if it has been a waste of time, time is my least concern. I have been absorbed for some hours and that is in itself worthwhile. Conceiving and carrying out any project at all is the only means I have to fill the interminable hours.

Perhaps I shall catch a fish. This is virgin territory; the fish might see no menace in the strange blue ribbon attached to a piece of mollusc. It is getting dark now. Soon there will be a moon. I have heard that moonlight is the ideal time for fishing. My bait is ready and my line is ready. I sit on the beach, listening to the sunset. How quiet it is. The movements of light and dark, the shadows and the melting distance, all are quiet. How can it be that there is so much motion without sound? Why, when dark and light meet on the golden horizon, is there so much glory of colour, hushed colour and gentle? Here I have beauty so untrammelled, so unmarred by intrusive noise that my soul is moved. I, who cried for sound, stand in wonder at soundlessness. There is peace, and philosophy pervades my brain. Thoughts of God and forevermore. And I, the great scorner of banality, steep myself in this beauty, this sunset that I would, in other times, have described as banal. There have been many sunsets here, just as glorious, which registered before only as casual appreciation, afflicted as I was with the hackneyed cynicism of my generation. It is a reflection, perhaps, of a new, developing attitude in me that I now can feel this beauty, hear it and know it deep inside me, as well as just looking at it.

As the sunset fades the silence remains. The lurking moon asserts its presence. It is too dark now to write. I am going fishing.

✵   ✵   ✵

Today I eat shellfish again. The fishing rig was the failure expected of it. Fish nibbled the bait constantly but, virgin territory or not, none was so foolish as to bite it. I rebaited four times, after which the hook fell into two pieces. I did consider using the pin of my belt buckle, but it is brass and much too soft. I believe Polynesian people make fish hooks out of shell. There must be a technique for it. I shall think about it.

The abalone shells are really very attractive. Inside they are grey and pink like mother of pearl, highly sheened and smooth as if purposely buffed to a lustre. Outside they are encrusted with hard deposits and algae, but I can remove this with the penknife. Beneath the deposits is a dark and beautiful carapace of blues and greens, sometimes with pink edges, sometimes white, black and even purple. The biggest one I have caught is over six inches broad and contained, I would think, half a pound of meat, but the big ones are relatively rare; they average about half that size in diameter and it takes three or four to make a decent meal. Actually, to make a decent meal in any gastronomic sense one has to slice them thinly – I do this with the honed edge of a shell – and pummel them to tenderness with a flat rock. But whatever I do now, the taste has become hateful. I shall have to cook them; I shall light a fire with coconut husks and fry them in coconut juice, using the large shell as a pan. One could consider it a waste of resources, catering only to indulgence, but I need something nice amidst this sterility, some encouragement, and it will give me a chance to smoke.

I remember my mother cooking bacon in a large, flat, cast-iron frying pan. Our house had a coke range which, so far as I can recall, was never allowed to go out, not in my youth, anyway. It was recessed into a wall, the only masonry wall in the house, and one had to take much care examining the pots on the range, because the recess was ringed with dangling ladles and saucepans ready to collide with great cheer into the head of any unwary invader. My mother was very short and even the most aggressive low-hung pot happily missed her head. She was not only short, she was stout. I remember her as grey and grim, which is an unfair memory, for she loved us all very much indeed, all three of her children. She worked continually from early morning to an unknown hour after our bedtime to ensure our comfort and content; but she spoke to us in constant scolds throughout the day. Cuddles were rare, at least I remember few, although I suppose as an infant I received my share. My mother, though unsmiling and sharp of voice, was essentially warm and full of her love for us; it was just that her affection was not external, although somehow we were always aware of it and sure of it. She spent a good deal of her life beside that cast-iron range, cooking, always cooking. I don't think she was a good cook by any means; she was basically a dumplings and porridge sort of mother, but she cooked bacon to perfection. My father was fond of bacon. He liked it for breakfast every morning that he was at home; not that he was at home most of the time. He was a commercial traveller and his domestic sojourns were fairly infrequent. I liked my father; he was a jolly man and tended to spoil his children. But I can't say I knew him well. He was of average height, average build, really a most average man. He had a moustache darker than his brown hair that came so far around his mouth, it completely separated his jaw from his upper face, and that was his most memorable feature; that and the fact that he liked bacon. My mother adored him. Not for him the grim visage, the sharp voice; for him she was soft, for him she reserved her smiles. I never knew them to quarrel. In my later years, with the unholy wisdom of maturity and with the bitterness that comes with knowing reality, I came to the conclusion that my father was completely unfaithful to her; that he wasn't a moral man. But perhaps it wasn't at all relevant, for what mattered was that my mother never knew, and he loved her when he was at home. Of course, I never really knew, either; my judgement is based entirely upon typecast association, and that isn't evidence. Still, I am sure of it.

The image of my mother scowling over her skillet is like a photograph on my memory. She doesn't move, she is two-dimensional, she is flat; a squat figure: full, wide buttocks, stockings rolled down to her calves, grimy toe projecting through her slippers, short arms thick like a butcher's, the frying pan, a great heavy cast-iron thing, like a trowel in her hands. Love overwhelms me. I am crying. My mother is old now and I haven't been to see her for more than a year. She shrivelled when my father died, travelling fast and almost drunk. Then the great range went out for the first time and my mother withered in her shell. I was away then. I was often away in those days, too often. I miss her now as I know she must have missed me then, and now, too. Dear Mother, I love you. I leaned on you in my growing and my youth, as later I leaned on the strength of Hugo and other friends. Was there not one person who leaned on me? Not Martine. Monique, perhaps, but I can't recall a single instance when I gave her strength; and yet . . . yet she would never have needed it. She was essentially a giving person herself; her need was for someone who needed her giving. For a time, that someone was me. It was a privilege I didn't recognise. Now there is none from whom to take such giving, as there is none on whom to lean. I love my mother more now, in absence and unattainability, than I ever loved her in the unquestioning acceptance of her industry and her sacrifice. The recognition that only my present utter aloneness induces the appreciation of her devotion is what depresses me. Would I never have realised the selflessness of her motherhood without this situation? Possibly, but not so profoundly. Oh, I ache for her as a child aches. I'm not a man, but a small boy needing comfort and arms about me, needing security, needing help.

Self-pity engulfs me.

I had some bad moments then. Still the residue is with me. I wanted to die. I ran the blade of my penknife up and down my wrists but without pressure. Withering cowardice maintains my existence. I threw the knife aside and masturbated violently. As always, that enhances depression. I am smoking now as I write; slowly the smoking and the writing are soothing me. I'm determined to indulge and smoke this cigarette to the end, thus exhausting half my stock. Why does one enjoy it? The taste is hardly pleasant. I can't relate it to suckling at a breast; drinking from a coconut is more palatable and more analogous to suckling, but far less satisfying. The reason for the enjoyment of this rumpled cigarette eludes me. Sufficient that I do enjoy it. It's nearly gone now. The tip burns my lips.

It is over, and regret arises. I feel emotions so clearly, more clearly than ever before in my life, so that it's possible to say, 'Now I feel this,' analytically and consciously as if I were a spectator of my own responses. One has always been aware of one's feelings, of course, and has acted because of them, but full awareness tended to be retrospective. One could say later, 'I regretted that,' but now I can say, 'This is regret,' as I feel it. I know how regret feels as it occurs, as I know, equally, that it will pass. It is even conceivable that I could wait for the moment of its going and record it. But it is too momentary. Already the regret has gone and I wasn't aware of its passing.

Depression, too, has lifted. I'm thirsty. There is still fresh water in the reservoir for I have been careful to conserve it. But it will be gone in two more days.

✻   ✻   ✻

49

Well, now I am proud, and with some justification this time. I've made a diving mask. This is an ingenuity which far out-strips my understood capacity, and it works, for I've already tried it. I commenced by fitting half a coconut husk to my face by careful paring with the penknife, then I cut two holes in which to fit the lenses from my spectacles; these holes were recessed and the lenses sealed against the recesses by means of elastic rings from my underpants. The fibrous material of the husk, though tough to cut, makes it fairly easy to wedge the lenses in place. Below them I made a slot through the face of the husk through which to slip my belt so that I can tighten the mask snugly, if a bit uncomfortably, against my face. It leaks, I admit that, but not enough to discomfort a single shallow dive. I have to drain it every time I surface, but that is of little consequence. I can swim on the surface for several minutes without much seepage at all, and a whole new range of food prospects has been revealed. There are other types of shellfish; there are lobsters, many more than I had previously realised; there are fish, free-swimming fish, fish in caves, fish almost everywhere, and there are turtles – one at least that I've seen.

So I am rightly proud of my inventiveness. Not only has the conception and the occupation kept me absorbed for two complete days, but the satisfaction from its success has kept my natural inclination to depression from taking hold. An optimism has grown within me, nursed and encouraged for the last few days. I have eaten well; cooked shellfish and lobster. Not yet fish, for it is apparent my spear needs added propulsion, but I think I've solved that problem. Today I shall catch a fish. My cooking is, by any standards, inadequate, but after eating raw shellfish for so long, any cooking at all is an improvement.

The lobsters have no claws and are easy to catch, although one must not pull them by their feelers or they are lost. They squeeze themselves into crevices and holes and one must grab them before they lodge tightly. They snap their abdomens onto one's fingers, but that does little damage apart from some minor scratching. I have caught three so far, one large enough for two or three meals; the flesh is very filling. But I want a fish.

I have tied the remnants of the elastic waistband from my underpants to the base of the spear, so that, when it is stretched up the spear and released, it will create a catapult effect. No doubt it is the success of my mask that has prompted my new surge of ingenuity, a belated ingenuity perhaps, but it isn't in my nature to be inventive as a matter of course. In normal living I accepted technology without more than token questioning, rarely bothering to examine the principles relating to function. Suffice it that gadgets worked. So my personal pride is exaggerated in proportion to my previous lack of self-reliance. This world, this dot of earth, is mine, for I have conquered it.

*   *   *

I wrote those last words with pride, and that pride, I believe, with some justice. But it was premature. I failed in my efforts to spear a fish. It is much more difficult than I had imagined. Several times I did manage to strike a fish tucked in a cave, but succeeded only in dislodging a few scales. There is still insufficient power in the spearing action, although I did actually succeed once in piercing a fish's flesh by trapping it against the side of a crevice and forcing my weight upon the spear. But I found I couldn't retrieve it without withdrawing the point. The moment I released the pressure the fish thrashed most powerfully and was gone, trailing blood. I conceded defeat. But I haven't conceded totally. I can improve the spear; it needs a barb, and practice will improve my technique.

*   *   *

I can't do it. I nearly drowned and I've lost my mask and the spear. Sixty seconds of disaster and my resources have vanished. And with my resources my self-confidence, which was such a fragile thing. I am a hollow shell. The shadows of defeat have eclipsed the tentative glimmer of optimism. Forever. Without the mask I can't make fire, I can't cook, I can't smoke. I dived and I dived and I dived to find the mask, and each time despair grew larger within me. Despair is not black, it isn't grey, it has no hue at all. It has only pain. It is nausea. What can I do? Oh, Christ! What can I do? Please help me! Help me!

That was perhaps my blackest moment, and in that statement I have given despair a hue. I resort to a cliché, but it is inadequate. There can be no word to convey such a nadir of being. I am surely above it now, but I feel that, in the shadows of the trees, are waiting the dreadful demons of abjection, the dispirits that are the remains of my soul, and I fear them. I don't want ever to experience such a phase again.

Yet it was so nearly success. I had the fish on my spear, tearing a hole in itself to escape the barb. I had already been down too long; I needed to breathe. I was tired and the mask was blurred with moisture. But I could not let it go. I slid my hands along the spear, my lungs pounding. I had to surface. Yet I was actually grasping the fish. Its strength was astounding. Air, I had to have air. The fish lunged. There was a shock against my face. My mask was gone. Where was the surface? There was water in my lungs. Somehow I reached the shore, coughing and retching and ill with fear. The mask. I had to get the mask.

I didn't get it. The mask is there somewhere on the sea bed, less than twenty feet deep. No. But of course, it floats. What a fool I am, what an inane, what an utter fool. The blasted thing is buoyant. Why didn't I realise that? My only excuse is the panic of the moment, an irrational, unthinking state of mind. The mask is there somewhere on the surface of the ocean, being gently rocked by the tides. I remember my frantic diving to retrieve the damned thing from the bottom, the desperate waste of energy, and that destructive thought erodes the faint new hope that the mask might yet float to shore. But the hope is there. I must consciously encourage it. Coconuts float, they drift to shore on the tide. It is not lost for ever. Already the shadows retreat.

It is too late now to search the shoreline. Dusk and the sunset are already apparent. When the moon is high and the beach is gentle, then I shall go down and wash in the moonbeams. There I shall meet my ladylove. She will be waiting, expecting me. Her bare feet will scuff the silver sand as she comes to meet me, her naked arms half raised, palms down, awaiting the touch of fingertips. Her hair will be golden and her eyes will be green. And she will sing for me. I shall be enveloped in music. And she will dance on that molten beach, wrapped in moonlight.

Ah, my love, I am coming. Soon I shall come.

✻　　✻　　✻

The mask has not floated to shore. However, the thought that it might has served to stimulate me, and I have managed to light a fire after all by using my watch glass. I had to break the watch to get the glass off, but keeping time is a most futile exercise. It isn't glass at all, really, merely a sort of plastic, but it served the purpose, and my confidence is a little higher because of it. I should have thought of it earlier, I suppose, but I have already made mention of my lack of natural resourcefulness. I wonder what other things I have failed to see.

I have read that Polynesians use the coconut tree for so many of life's basic needs; I believe they even make cloth with it, although that particular talent wouldn't be of much help to me. How much could I do with it, though, if I had more knowledge? I use the milk for refreshment, the flesh for food, the shell for a utensil and the husk for fuel. I hope to use the fronds later for thatching, but they serve as covers for my reservoirs which are empty at the moment. Even so, the supply of coconuts is limited. If I used only one coconut per day, my stock would be exhausted within a fortnight. They do seem to regenerate themselves quite rapidly, but the rate is not enough to encourage anything but the severest rationing. I use them more for drink than for food, in fact, for the juice is much more palatable when the meat is undeveloped, and I am becoming quite expert at judging the most prime nut for my purpose.

I dived today without the mask. It was necessary more to regain my confidence in the water than for any need of food. Prior to the loss of my mask I was growing extremely confident, diving further and further from shore and at increasing depths. I didn't dive more than about twenty feet because the mask leaked too much at that pressure, but I was finding that I could stay under for longer periods than in my early days. Of course, the mask was itself responsible for this increased capacity, vision giving me stimuli as well as a reduction in natural apprehension. Today that apprehension was very evident and deliberate control had to be exercised. Imagination creates more terrors than reality, and uses up more air. On the north side of the island the bottom slopes gently for the first fifty yards or so – I haven't ventured any further – and is mainly of similar basic material to the shore: soft rock but with less sand and a variety of submarine growth, more dense in patches where the rock is broken up to form small reefs. The east and west sides are much the same but the depth increases dramatically at about thirty yards offshore. The southern end is far more rocky, less vegetated, and the currents there are strong. After an initial exploration I haven't dived there again.

Today the sea is flat. The weather is flat. Everything is flat. The feeling comes upon me that a boat will appear across the flatness. It is so strong a feeling that I have sat for hours staring at the horizon. And that has given me a headache; it was a foolish activity, in fact an inactivity, but the headache is the first I have suffered here and I am sure it will soon pass.

One gets used to boredom. It becomes a strange sort of lack of expectancy. Sometimes time drifts over me as I sit or lie in the shade of the palm trees. I masturbate frequently, no longer allowing any shade of self-disgust to affect my following mood, content to enjoy the carnal pleasure for its own sake as a small purpose in a purposeless being. Once I carved the letter 'J' into the bark of the odd tree, but found that to be a totally uninspiring occupation where no occupation at all would not be worse. It smacked of mutilation, a sort of vandalism, and I regret it. There are times, increasingly frequent, when I seem to lose time altogether. It isn't sleep, but I'm not aware of wakefulness. I don't feel sensation then. I don't think. I just lie and the hours ignore me. The will to move, to act, actually to think, deserts me. I can't see that it matters. The standards of my early existence have no meaning. There are no morals here, for morals depend upon social interaction, and because there are no morals there cannot be guilt. Terms like laziness, selfishness, sloth, cowardice, self-abuse, terms that are derogatory or contemptuous in organised society – and I deem rightly so – become utterly without value in isolation such as mine. They are terms reflecting social judgements, entirely dependent upon comparison with other people. Without other people, they have no meaning. Now that I have come to understand that, guilt does not assail me, but in truth it did bother me previously, conditioned as I was to the values of another existence. It is only recently that the total invalidity of those concepts has dawned upon me. Is that an excuse for myself? Of course it is. But who is my prosecutor? Who accuses me? Only my own indoctrinated conscience. Perhaps during this period of my isolation, indoctrination can be erased and I can think out new parameters of truth.

My last cigarette has gone. I am going to give up smoking.

*   *   *

'There you are,' said the old man, 'the sea has given it back to you.'

'Yes,' I said. The mask rolled onto the sand. The waves nudged it towards my feet as if saying: 'See, I have brought it back.' I watched it, not deigning to pick it up.

The old man shifted on the rock upon which he was perched. 'You must have faith,' he said.

'Where's the girl?' I asked.

He shrugged his shoulders so that he looked like a condor. He was very thin and he looked ridiculous in his striped nightshirt. His eyelids sagged away from his eyes so that, whatever his mouth did, he couldn't smile. His chin was

55

covered in stubble. The sea continued to make its offering, persisting gently.

'You must be uncomfortable there,' I remarked.

'Is comfort so important?' His voice was quiet, polite.

'But of course. Lack of it is my main tribulation.' We were both silent then. I stirred some wet sand with my toe. 'I imagine the whole of man's life is really a search for greater comfort.'

'Not wealth?' he questioned.

'Only as a means to additional comfort.'

He stood up. The nightgown seemed to hang on him as if from drawing pins. 'I find that an intolerable idea,' he said. He came close and grasped my elbow with a hand that was all bones. It was an extraordinarily powerful grip. 'Is comfort your highest priority here? Wouldn't you sacrifice what little you have for one hour, half an hour, ten minutes, even, spent with the girl, the real girl in the flesh?'

'That's an unfair question,' I retorted. 'My circumstances are quite different from the standard.'

'Ah! but is it not deprivation that gives true value to be-haviour and the needs of mankind?'

I should know him. There is something about him that is familiar. 'No, not at all,' I replied, 'deprivation exaggerates need, and therefore values.'

'But here you have no exaggeration. You have only the most fundamental requirement: that of nourishment.'

'I have other requirements, I just don't have opportunities to satisfy them.'

'Exactly. You have no music, for example, no company, and only the most meagre degree of comfort. You are in a unique position to establish priorities.'

The sea still washed the mask, not moving it higher, but reluctant to forsake it finally. 'Sex is not my first priority,' I said, squatting and scooping furrows with my fingers. The old man was now gripping my shoulder.

He said: 'Love, though.' It was a statement rather than a question.

My heart was aching with loneliness. 'Some sort of company. Just someone to talk to, that's all. Not necessarily a girl.'

I picked up the mask and examined it. It seemed undamaged. The lenses were still in place and unbroken and the belt was still threaded through its slot. I became conscious that the pressure of his hand was absent and I realised that he had left me. Perhaps I had offended him, whoever or whatever he was.

I put the mask in a place beyond the reach of the tide and walked along the beach. Slowly. I walked round the island four times before morning. She didn't come.

✻   ✻   ✻

Another night. So many. So interminable. Have I a future? Is there a world out there? The moon glitters like an Arab scimitar. This island is gifted with more stars than any other spot on Earth. Every night I see them in that same position. Reason tells me that that is a fallacy. My eyes refute the fallacy. The only change is the moving stars, and there are many of those, many many more than I ever saw at home. What are they? Are they comets? Space ships? Fantasy can capture me.

'They are space ships,' murmurs the old man from behind me.

'Meteorites,' I state firmly, not turning round.

'The space ships burn up when they enter the atmosphere,' he carries on as if I had not spoken.

'The fragments that have been collected are made of rock,' I tell him, not really wishing to pursue the fantasy.

'Iron and silica, mostly. The elements used in the fabric of space ships.'

'Silica? Do they use silica in spaceships?' I turn and face him.

'Why not?' He is still clothed in that ridiculous nightshirt, but he has added a nightcap. He looks even more comic. 'Who knows what they use? Who understands alien technology?' He persists with the fantasy, but the mood for enigmatic nonsense has left me.

'Go away,' I say, and he goes immediately. I must ask him for his name.

57

I found a turtle on the beach this afternoon and caught it without undue fuss; it couldn't escape me out of its element. I turned it onto its back. It's still there, still alive, its flippers swimming slowly in the air, in unison, uselessly. It must be a cruelty to leave it thus. Why am I cruel to it? Why does it give me so little concern? Have I lost my compassion with my guilt? Can I eat it? How do I kill it? How do I dismember it? I'll solve those problems. I'll sleep now and think about them in the morning. The carapace should be useful.

✳   ✳   ✳

There is in this solitude a complete dependency upon one's mood which in turn is affected by the small successes or failures that in other circumstances would be insignificant. Because of this, one becomes sharply aware of one's mood, and if it seems to be depressive, or even too elative, one must consciously try to alter it. But the diversions are limited. One cannot control mood by will alone, although I try. I play mental games, and of course I write my thoughts down, deliberately, as if I anticipated someone would read them one day. That is improbable and I realise it, and, really, there are parts of this writing that I would prefer to delete, being too personal for public assessment; but for now, with the unlikelihood of it ever being made public, I shall write as I feel, for that is the greatest aid I have towards mood control.

One was educated to believe that in solitude there is peace, and when solitude is voluntary and the duration of it subject to personal decision, the concept is undoubtedly true. Well, there is peace here, continuous, monotonous, unvarying peace; the only aggression is the occasional violence of the elements, and even that has been of the mildest form so far. However, that is a limited peace, a physical peace; it isn't the peace for which one would search in society. Solitude here is the reverse of that peace, it is an agony, of mind and of emotion. There is a horror in total quiet that has to be experienced to be understood, a total quiet that lasts day after day after day. I have seen birds here, and they have squawked and quarrelled together, but even that is rare. I long for the songs of woodland birds. There was a period in my youth when I was wakened daily in a scout camp by the carolling of a lark, and one could not ask for a more thrilling start to a day. And I have heard nightingales and stood rapt in the unbelievable trilling of their unseen joy. I yearn for those sounds, just sparrows twittering and scuffling in the hedgerows, common sounds, so ordinary as to be scarcely heard, only recognised in absence.

And not only birds; the music of children playing, of cows calling to be milked, the rustles of mysterious creatures in the grass. If one had these things with solitude, then perhaps one could obtain a greater degree of peace, for peace is not a virgin fabric, it needs the myriad interruptions to evenness to make it endurable.

٭ ٭ ٭

I've finally caught a fish. Already I have cooked it and eaten it. I did that almost immediately, and it must have been the most satisfying meal of my life; not only was it tasty, it has done wonders for my confidence. It was in fact an absurdly easy accomplishment. Today I elected to swim over the sandy bottom rather than the more prolific rocky areas. The sea is particularly flat and clear today, and the shape of the fish was readily distinguished in the sand. I had only a short pointed stick with me to replace my spear, but it was a simple matter to dive and skewer the fish in one movement. The water was less than six feet deep. I forced the stick through it and into the sand beneath, and almost in the same motion let one hand go to regrasp the stick below the fish. It could not escape, and the effort was minimal. Now that I have the technique, I should be able to eat fish regularly, but I must adjust to eating it raw. Scarcity of fuel is beginning to be a problem, and paper to light it with will soon be exhausted. The method of lighting needs paper. I don't know what I could use as a substitute.

Sometimes it is so cold at night, when the wind blows from

59

the south, that I am tempted to light a fire for warmth. I must resist that. It is necessary to ration my comforts meticulously. Coconuts, fire and my pencils. The pencils are lasting well; I keep the points short. That technique is possibly the only one of any use that I brought with me to the island; all others had to be learned. Someone with more knowledge of sea things and coconut trees, and with more natural invention, might have done better than I, but I have achieved survival. I can drink and I can eat; not much else, but I need not die. And I think that I've retained my sanity; there have been aberrations, but on the whole I am still rational. Apart from the cold at nights and recently a tooth starting to be worrisome, life here must now be at its optimum potential for comfort. There appear to be no more possibilities. There are the birds, of course. It might be feasible to devise a method of ensnaring one, but for what purpose? The food resources that I have must surely be more desirable than the flesh of an oily seabird. There is the turtle. It is dead now and I didn't have to kill it. Soon I shall commence the task of dismemberment.

I feel my mind is especially lucid now. Analytical. I read my recorded conversations with the old man and ponder on that effect of my need without ridicule. Who was he? What was he in my past? Why this conjunction of absurdity and philosophy? My memory refuses to recall him. Perhaps he didn't exist as I see him now; perhaps he is a combination of many personalities. The girl, of course, needs no logic. She is just the personification of my physical requirements. I never talk to her. I never touch her; I just see her. She isn't Martine, or Monique, or a mixture of them. She is no girl I ever knew. I call her Deirdre, for no other reason than that I like the name. She is a romantic illusion, and it needs no special insight to realise that. But the old man must be considered differently; he is hardly a romantic illusion. He is real. He has flesh and he touches me. Why have I chosen an old man in a nightshirt for a companion? There must be something in my psyche that establishes the type and form of my illusions, but what it is, is too complex for my understanding.

I wonder what I can do with the turtle shell. It must have some practical use.

* * *

It is wet tonight and windy, and I am miserable. Not depressed, just miserable. I am used to being wretched now and accept it. It isn't exactly stoicism, more a plateau of condition upon which I can remain with a certain security; before, misery was a prelude to despair, a mental slope where, unless I found a footing of determination, I would slide rapidly into self-pity. My reservoirs will be full in the morning; I have four now, including the inverted carapace. That is one consolation for this remorseless discomfort. My tooth is bothering me, from the cold, I expect. I pray that it gets no worse. I could hardly die of toothache, but it is the thought that there would be no possibility of relief that is the danger. That could jar my mental equilibrium beyond repair. I see that my grip on sanity is sometimes tenuous indeed, and assuredly it is the writing that reinforces it. Toothache could be the one factor likely to loosen that tenuous grip. Yet what is my criterion for sanity? Can I be my own judge of my mental condition?

The wind is too strong for writing.

* * *

Two days have passed. There was a storm. I cannot recall a more dreadful experience in my whole life. It was so cold I thought that I had to die. I shivered continually for a full twenty-four hours. The wind raged beyond human comprehension. I could only lie face downwards in the futile shelter of the trees. I was hit on the hip by a falling coconut, and for a while I believed my hip was smashed. It is not the case, but the pain remains. There isn't a coconut left on the trees, and only the skimpiest foliage. It will take months for them to recover, and one of my important resources has gone. It is still cold and the wind continues, but less violently, and the rain has stopped. I am thoroughly wet. There is nothing dry with which to light a fire except perhaps the innermost pages of this book. I shall not use those, even if there were sufficient to achieve more than a momentary flame when the sun finally appears. That would seem unlikely for some time.

I am determined to survive. I think of the possibility of pneumonia but refuse to acknowledge it. I have eaten some raw turtle meat and a coconut. This island will not kill me. One day I shall be found. I shall be sane and I shall be strong. That is my resolve. It was the purpose that enabled me to last out the storm. I lay shivering under the shrieking trees, while the demented wind and the rain pounded at my body, huddled and powerless; and then the resolution came. It was a strength of purpose such as I have never had, that I was previously unaware that I could feel. Surely isolation has given me this will. I have learned determination. I am shivering still, but I think the storm is over. Sooner or later the sun will come out and there will be warmth. I shall be dry. I need no one; no man, nor woman. I stand alone. I am strong. Undefeated. I shall not be battered.

✻   ✻   ✻

I am a king. I am a king without subjects, but the trees and the beach are mine to command.

'Are you not rather a subject without a king?' The old man's voice comes from the beach below me. I can't see him.

I laugh. 'King. Subject. What relevance have they here? Status is as meaningless as crime.'

'Is crime ever meaningless?' I still can't see him. His voice is sharp, however; he sounds close enough to be seen.

'Crime is a social concept, a social sin.'

'Not a sin of your conscience?'

'These are stupid questions, old man. You can't judge me by the values of another world. Show yourself, I want to know who you are.'

Silence, lasting so long I'm tempted to rise and seek him. Instead I write. I'm not troubled by the lingering tendrils of conscience his questions represent. They are the dying sallies of indoctrination. I can commit no crime here.

'You can't deny your genetic make-up.' He comes from the darkness but stands still in shadow. And I know him. That is an exact statement from my childhood. He is my schoolteacher, Muller.

'I know you,' I say. 'You're much older and you wear that silly nightshirt, but I know you.'

'I was wearing it when I died,' he says flatly.

So now I am clear. He was one of the major instruments in the shaping of the conscience that is now twitching before final extinction. It isn't strange that he hovers as the spectre of what once was. Comic now. As irrelevant as the inculcation of his discipline. He is truly representative of something dead.

'Social conscience is necessary for the ordered functioning of any society.' The exact phrase. Long forgotten insistencies from the classroom. I smell it now, the carbolic and the chalk. I hear the shuffles of unstill shoes, the sniffling, the constant sniffling. I recall one girl who always sniffled, and even her name comes back – Anna Tims. The memories are lucid. She had dark untidy hair, kept in futile pigtails with torn strips of pink cotton knotted unevenly and grey with grime. She was thin and her face was blotchy with her pubescence. The boys would pay her sweets or stolen cigarettes so that she would pull down her knickers in the locker room just to let them look. For money she would allow them to touch her with a finger. I wonder what became of her. She held little interest for me and, once our mixed classroom days were over, her existence became meaningless. For me. Frank told me she went on to a convent. I remember her merely as the one who sniffled most. Or was it Jenny who went on to the convent? I liked Jenny. She dug a pencil in my leg; there is a graphite mark there to this day.

'Without society there's no need for conscience,' I state.

'But you have to maintain your standards for when you return to society.'

'You are my hope, then, as well as my conscience.'

63

'It is only your own hope that you hear.'

'You were always a platitudinous bastard.'

The desk was perched clumsily on a raised area of the floor too small for the burden, so that Muller constantly had to step up and down as he strutted about during his teaching efforts. The old scratched blackboard, more grey than black with ingrained chalk, hung wearily behind the desk, the ledge in front cluttered with bits of chalk and two ineffectual felt dusters. But it was that old blackboard that gave me the foundation of all that I have learned. Futile erudition. Though it could not always have been Muller. Was it ever?

He used to rap the blackboard with a ruler. He emphasised facts with that ruler, those implacable, demonstrable facts and that irrefutable mathematics. But truth is so much more than mathematics.

'You mustn't compare mathematics with philosophy.'

'I seek truth, old man. You are not truth. You are an illusion.'

He is a composite of my need for company and the memories of youth; but the memories themselves are part illusion, so distorted by the recreation of them and fused with so many intrusive scenes from later life, stories read and pictures seen, that what is truth in them cannot be disseminated.

My tooth is aching again.

*   *   *

The sky is gloriously blue once more. I have stored all the fallen coconuts. With those and my covered reservoirs I have plenty to drink for some time; the coconuts are too green to serve as food. It appears that my diet is adequate, however; I am really remarkably healthy. Except for this damned tooth. I don't know what to do about it. It's a molar, so there's no chance of devising a technique to remove it. I caught a fish again today. I was foolish to throw the skeleton of the previous one away. Surely fish bones will make spear barbs and fish hooks. I must experiment.

The storm has blown down eleven palm fronds which now cover my reservoirs; but later, as the water is used up, I shall use them to fashion a shelter. They last for many weeks before degenerating into brittle uselessness.

Apart from the novel, I have hardly any paper left, but I have succeeded in getting a flame to start on the dried palm fronds by application of unusual patience. Fuel is becoming very scarce and my rationing has to be severe. There are only old coconut husks and green boughs from the odd tree which I'm most reluctant to use. I eat raw food mostly, but I shall cook my fish.

It's evening now. The moon is so bright that I can write as easily as in daylight. The fish was delicious. I took pains to cook it thoroughly, knowing the extravagance but needing some compensation for the misery of the last two days. I have been alert since the storm; there has been no loss of hours, no drifting into mindless lethargy. Tonight my toothache has subsided. I know it's there but it isn't insistent.

How long have I been here? This beautiful evening sky should provide a clue, but I can't recognise it as different from when I came. It must be, of course. I should have plotted it, marked it on the sand as it was then. But it didn't occur to me to do so. Hugo would have done that; he would have seen it as a fundamental procedure. He would have collected a stone or shell each day to record the passage of time. It does seem that often the basics and the obvious escape me, at least when it's most useful to see them. But I'll do it now, record the sky on the beach with stones and shells, then repeat the exercise every twenty-eight days. The concept excites me. I am eager to begin, so eager that I have to exercise restraint. It is a project. I need such a stimulus to my sluggish intellect as much as I need sustenance. The restraint is also a pleasure to be savoured. Here, where time has no meaning, such impatience can be the substance of meditation. Such possibilities must be cherished, rationed as a resource. Writing now is a deliberate effort to subdue the impatience, but I still see relevance in it. Two factors are apparent: because time is without meaning, what is the need to hurry? The sky will certainly change, but not greatly over a few nights. And because of the meaninglessness of time, the project itself can have no meaning. Yes, it will be an irrelevant record of passing months, but so important for the vital element of occupation.

Occupation is the mainstay of my sanity. I claim that I am sane now, but if it were otherwise, could the mad judge the degree of madness? I worry about that. Needlessly, perhaps, for my degree of sanity or insanity affects only me. Even if I were to be rescued, any strangeness in my character would be rationalised. I shan't concern myself with the question now. But I do need this intellectual stimulus.

*   *   *

It is done. It was a most difficult exercise. Thankfully, it was difficult. I have been thoroughly absorbed for two nights, absorbed in the geometry of the heavens, in the problems of scale and angle. Fascinated. So conscious of celestial detail, and becoming equally conscious of self. It has been the most marvellous period of my enforced hermitage, enthralling not only in the doing of it, but in the realisation that there can be relief from the corrosive tedium. For a while, during the concentration and the rapture, I felt that I was close to a wisdom, a wisdom so profound that, had I grasped it, an infinite clarity of understanding would have been mine; the wisdom of all men, of all time, of all gods. Somehow it eluded me. Perhaps in my sudden awareness of its proximity. There was an instant when I waited for it to pervade me. That was an exquisite moment. A moment of calm and peace and expectancy. And though there was no insight, neither was there disappointment, there was no anticlimax. The peace remained, and the mental record of the moment. I understand why the stars have so captivated the minds of men throughout history; Galileo, Aristotle, maybe they grasped their moments of wisdom where mine slipped past.

I am proud of my effort on the beach. Photographically the proportions would not be right; one cannot encompass the immense scope of heaven on a few square yards of sand. But I like it. I have looked at it many times in admiration, like a schoolboy looks again and again at his first efforts at art, and believes it to be good. I believe my effort is good. I think it's excellent. I'll have to ask Muller what he thinks, although he hasn't appeared since I discovered his identity.

I acknowledge that his identity is an aspect of my own subconscious being and, in recognising that, perhaps I have precluded any further embodiment of the old man. I do hope not. The girl I haven't seen for a week or two. That is less important.

I am very hairy now; my beard is long and itches far less than during its early growth, a matted fuzz full of sand and salt, and thick like my hair; they are both brown, still, and thriving, though I wish it were otherwise. Hair causes my mask to leak. But I am in amazingly good health, despite the limitations of my diet, and fit, too, for exercise and swimming are my only pastimes. This blasted tooth is the sole intrusion into my physical well-being. It isn't too bad at this moment.

I have become basically a nocturnal creature, although I dive in the mornings for my larder. Most of the day I sleep. The moon is so bright at night that I can roam the beach with little impairment to vision, usually looking for another turtle. I've seen them occasionally in the sea, but they need to be on shore for me to be able to catch them. Yet there are crabs to catch, some as big as my hand. I rarely wear clothes now, except when the weather is unusually cool. I walk naked, completely naked, as naked and hairy as my most primitive forebear, with such improved speed and agility that I could probably match that forebear in the quest for food. Few opportunities pass me now for catching sea creatures either in or out of the water, and I have worked on the mask, and worked on it again, and again and again, for many hours over many days; it fits my face so well and the lenses are so well sealed that it only leaks when I dive deep, and only then because of intrusive hair. Why should

67

I not be arrogant? I have developed the attributes needed to survive. So I am arrogant and I strut about till laughter disturbs the pomposity. But I have to beware of laughter, even though it is precious in itself; laughter is a difficult achievement on one's own. Yet it can be a danger. In the recognition of the ridiculous is the recognition of futility, the futility of arrogance without a foil, and that cognisance can be the seed of despair.

Despair is less common to me now, but hope, too, must be subdued, for to allow free rein to hope – any hope other than as a final outcome, as if my life here was a book to be read with the end hidden, distant even, but decided – would be like rocking a pendulum. Hope would inevitably be followed by despair. The achievement of equilibrium is a technique of my survival, but one I must never take for granted; it is the balance between the two poles that has to be cultivated. The more even the emotional plane, the more obvious the waiting phantoms of insanity.

I enjoyed plotting the stars so much, I see it as important to plan other cerebral exercises; I cannot always retreat into writing. Sooner or later the pages will be full, or my lead will be exhausted. There is plenty yet, but always I must conserve.

*   *   *

There are no birds today. The only living things on land within the compass of the horizon are the trees and myself, and maybe a few unseen crabs. Before the trees, this island must have been desolate indeed. How did they arrive? The coconuts came first; the other tree would need their humus to grow at all, although its roots must be in the sand. Coconuts float, of course, and even commence germination in the sea, I understand. These palms are all roughly the same height, so probably are all the one age. It would be reasonable to assume they all arrived on the same tide, unless they are the issue of one tree. The grove is at the highest point on the island, where normal tides don't reach, so either a single tree with fruit on it or six individual nuts were thrown high up in a storm. I haven't encountered such a storm, even the terrible one of a few days ago did not force the sea so high, so thankfully such storms are an extreme, rarely experienced. Otherwise the odd tree could not have grown.

The rationale that six nuts arrived here together, either loose or still attached to a parent tree, excites me quite out of proportion to the logic involved, for it would suggest another island within reasonable proximity; for although coconuts can float for thousands of miles, a group of them would surely become separated, and a tree would not travel far. The island of origin would have to be bigger than this one and already stocked with palm trees. I wonder just how close it is. Could I fell these trees and devise a raft? How would I hold the logs together? In what direction would I head? No, the thought is futile, an irrational surge of hope that must be discouraged. This is the over-riding logic: the palm trees, though barren now, are my most valuable resource; even if I could invent a means to fell them, and it could be done with shell and ingenuity, such an action would be total folly. The assumption that another island lies close by is based on the flimsiest reasoning, and although the prevailing currents might give a hint of direction, the range would be too vast for possibility. Oh, it is absurd, but the hope will not die.

Consider the other tree. There is a mystery. Its identity is an enigma; its being is miraculous, a tribute to resilience and the will to live, although in truth it hasn't done it too well. It is stunted, twisted with undernourishment, wretched in suffering; for it does suffer, that poor tree, a picture of pathos where the coconuts strut in arrogant possession. They belong; the other tree is a captive of incorrect ecology, a victim of vagrant germination. But what brought the seed? Was it birds? Or was it brought by human hand? I imagine some wandering canoe, or even a yacht, a launch, some passing ship, seeking shelter during a storm, or simply visiting the island from curiosity. There is only one attraction on the island, the grove of coconuts, and a man stands beneath them eating a fruit. Is the odd tree a fruit tree? It could be. I like the theory, for it encourages the flame of hope, and that hope is even less rational than the one before. The tree is a little taller than me, with a few scrawny boughs that are surprisingly supple and resinous. It drops its leaves quickly and I think before they really mature; but it doesn't have many. They are long and ovate in shape, initially red but turning soon to green. I have seen no signs of buds or flowers. It looks best after rain; it must rely on rainfall much more than the coconuts. I have an affinity with it; I, too, am a captive removed from my proper environment. We suffer together, the odd tree and I.

*   *   *

Even in this barren existence it is possible to glean moments of pure pleasure. Pleasures more enduring than carnal or cerebral ones; deeply felt, aesthetic, leaving satisfaction impregnated into one's tissues, so that the residual pleasure caresses the senses long after the wonder of the original, like the memory of a great concert. Today was wonderful. It is still the same day for there are many hours yet till evening, but it's time now to doze. I am a creature of the night and my limbs are tired. Gratifyingly tired.

Early this morning I went swimming as is my routine. Routine is itself important. I was looking for a lobster. The sea was very calm, virtually flat, and also very clear. Just swimming and observing was a pleasure. I have developed a technique of swimming in a slow, frog-like stroke, arms and legs moving in unison, turning my head every few seconds to breathe. The mask doesn't leak on the surface. The water was so pleasant, so clear, that I made no effort to dive and seek my lobster. There was no urgency. My life has no urgencies. The fish were unalarmed.

The sea bottom is as familiar to me now as the island. There is the rock that looks like a broken leg; over there on my left is the 'cairn'; now, my favourite place, the 'grotto'. In their clarity and their familiarity there was a small delight. Near the 'grotto' lives a red spotted fish, as long as my arm, with a blunt head and teeth exposed, startling white teeth that give him an aggressive look. But he is friendly, and always, whenever I cross his territory, he swims ahead of me; he has an amazing ability to predetermine my movements, so that, no matter where I veer off to, he still maintains that position three feet before my nose. He, too, was a small delight, a companion who was not an embodiment of my subconscious. He would leave me as surely as if he had struck an electric fence when he reached the limits of his territory. I know those limits now as well as he. Today I cruised behind him for several minutes, then veered off over the weed patch where I knew he wouldn't go. Just beyond the weed patch there is a sandy stretch about eighteen feet deep, but getting progressively deeper as it slopes away from the island. This was the limit of my own territory.

Then I saw another fish. An absolutely beautiful fish. Its colours were ordinary enough, just white and black vertical stripes, but its beauty was in its design. About as big and round as a dinner plate in its body, but with very large matching triangular fins, dorsal and anal, curving backwards and tipped with long, trailing streamers, duplicated from the tips of its tail. It was so extraordinarily lovely that I stopped swimming just six feet above it and gazed with an emotion close to disbelief. It was quite undisturbed by my presence and my adoration, and I was able simply to stare in astonishment as it hovered almost motionless by the slightest movements of those wonderful fins. Its mouth looked exactly as if it were blowing a tiny bugle, really comically small for so large a fish; I can't imagine what it would eat through so tiny a mouth or how it would obtain enough to sustain its bulk. After a few minutes it moved off. Enraptured, I followed it, the fact that it was luring me deeper only registering as inconsequential information submerged beneath the delight of the moment. It moved slowly and I had no trouble at all keeping it in view. I recorded that the bottom was getting more and more distant, but the water was so clear I could still see the details of the sea floor; it was sand, with a form of sea grass stubbled over it. Suddenly the fish changed direction and moved too swiftly for me to keep up, as if it had

71

taken flight. The thought of sharks hit me for the first time. For an instant I was overtaken by a flash of panic, but there were other fish in view now and they seemed unalarmed. My common sense asserted itself and I looked carefully around. Just ahead was a reef I had never seen before. I looked back. From the surface of the sea the beach appeared a long way away; still, the reef was only a few yards ahead and the whole place was as placid and unmenacing as a garden lawn. I decided to explore it.

What an exhilarating discovery. This reef was teeming with fish. Large fish, larger than I had seen anywhere on the closer reefs; glorious, multicoloured fish; long thin fish; globular fish; eels, lobsters, huge shellfish, small shellfish, octopi, sea urchins, starfish, creatures like massive slugs, crabs. So many living things. I could recognise the type of some, such as 'this is a crab', or 'that is a clam', but identification of the majority was beyond my limited knowledge. I lost track of time. I was completely absorbed in discovery, in the contemplation of this untouched loveliness. I was enchanted. I would be there still, but a wind arose and the sea grew ruffled. I had to empty the mask too often for comfort. With the thought that the reef would be there tomorrow, and always beyond, I returned to shore. It seemed a long swim back. I made myself tired and I caught no lobster. But the pleasure remains.

*   *   *

I call it Reef Four. I swam out there again today. The sea was not as calm and there was a current across the sandy area which made the swim more tiring than yesterday. But again I became lost in wonder. I took a stick with me with the intention of spearing a fish; they are so utterly without fear there. Yet I didn't do so. Part of the fascination of the place is the tranquillity of the whole biological system. It would be an act of murder to fracture it. My reason tells me that that concept is an absurdity. Death and mutilation are part of the total fabric of any living system; I know that, but I haven't seen it there.

'So you do have a concept of crime, even here?' Muller sits beside me, still in his nightgown. I don't answer him and he goes away. But the question lingers. It disturbs me. It seems that indoctrinated patterns of attitude still control my behaviour. Yes, I would consider it a criminal act to kill a fish on Reef Four, yet not elsewhere. Why is that? It is because the place is an entity for me as it is; it is the one place I can visit for no other reason than for pleasure. I don't need to kill there; my food can be readily obtained in some other place. Which means that I have developed a code of conduct, laws governing my actions. I have established the notion of bad acts. Cutting down a coconut palm would be a bad act. Killing on Reef Four would be a bad act. So, from the choking roots of indoctrination has arisen the shoot of a new morality. It has little relationship with my old concept of crime, and in those old terms there is no possible sin. In the old terms I can do no evil. I can do no good, either. I can harm or help no one but myself, and on whatever act I commit there can be no other judgement than my own.

Here, on my island, the world is irrelevant. If every human being elsewhere were destroyed in one unimaginable cataclysm, it would not affect my existence here in any conceivable way. If I knew of it, it would affect my buried hopes of rescue and by so doing would surely affect my attitude to existence, but as I could never know of it, that effect can only be an academic consideration. I cannot conceive of politics here, of people striving to arrange social order to their own advantage. I cannot conceive of the hopeless existence of slum dwellers, ghetto dwellers, of starving children, of criminals serving life sentences. Their existences, however impoverished or agonised or screamingly tormented, are theirs; so separate from mine that their anguish has no impact at all, as the anguish of a crushed beetle has no impact for anyone, as the distress of a hare torn apart by foxes has no meaning for man. My tooth is aching, it is aching with insistence, but its insistence has no meaning, no impact on any person but me. It is an unbearable pain, yet I will bear it, for there is no other course.

Too choppy today for visiting Reef Four. Already there are signs of new coconuts on the palm trees; it is quite amazing how quickly they develop.

My tooth is throbbing continually. My equilibrium wavers. I feel desperate. I want to knock the tooth out and would do that if there was any way it could be done. I realise the threat this pain can be to my stability of mind. I need mental occupation. I shall devise a chess set.

Occupation certainly helps. I chew on bits of palm leaves and convince myself that that helps, too. The thought that I am doing something strengthens me.

My chess set is made of shells. Large, cone-shaped shells for the kings and queens, differentiated by colour and size; smaller rounded shells, which I think are cowries, for the bishops; snails for the knights and small cones for the rooks. The pawns are respectively white and black halves of the many bivalve shells from the beach. The board is an area of sand marked out with the sinews from coconut fronds weighted with stones to hold them in place. Making the board and searching out the various shell types was diverting, but it is so difficult actually to play oneself. One cannot adopt a bias, but always knows the exact strategy of the opposition. The game progresses slowly, and I am becoming bored with it. That is not a good sign.

I long to go to Reef Four. The longing is not so different from the longing one feels for a mistress. It is my solace. I think constantly of it; the place where my troubles are soothed and peace prevails, a place of beauty and pleasure and bewitchment. Did I think of Martine like that? Oh yes, I'm sure I did. I would think of her during my daily tasks, just enduring till the moment of seeing her again. It was a yearning, a yearning without the interference of reason; in fact quite unreasonable. Then she was the pinnacle of all desire, but in recollection she was a singularly plain girl. Untidy. Breastless. She had a mole on the side of her nose, and pale, as pale as if she had spent her life in a cell, and she was very thin. Short dark hair, straight, cut off at a level just below her ears with an indeterminate parting in the middle. And large dark eyes that pulled the skin tight on her cheekbones; her allure was in her eyes. She had perfect teeth, I remember that. I recall the thin lips that I loved; her sensuality was not in her lips but I loved them.

Why did I love her? What was her particular magic for me? She was wild in her lovemaking. I remember her frenzy still with astonishment. Yet I think I loved her before I knew the passion of her. Still she is not complete. I knew her intimately but did I know her at all? There is some essence of her that escapes me now as it escaped me then. I wonder if she had an essence. Perhaps what I knew was all she was. A rather grubby, rather unhappy, rather wanton, restless creature, destined only for greater unhappiness. Was she wanton? For me, for one short period of time, she was wanton. But there was a shyness about her, a reticence with men, almost a chastity. Oh, what are you, Martine? Where are you? Were you real, or are you just another figment, another distortion of memory? Why is your image so flat? Are all men's memories just cardboard cutouts, two-dimensional snapshots with lifeless grins and static posture? Where is the motion? Where are the sounds of life? Where are the glints of the eyes and the quirks of the mouth and the gestures of hand? Where are the voices? I can't remember voices. Each voice has a timbre of its own, a particular inflection that distinguishes it from all others, and not one can I recall. I can't recall my mother's voice. I know her words, I know her phrases. Where is her voice?

Yet I do remember sounds. Music is still clear in my mind. Even now I can hear it. Piano music. Mozart. It comes from the south-east, the notes rising and falling with the waves. My mind is translating the wash of the sea into melody. Music is another longing, more deeply felt than strident lust, and now, almost, I have the reality of it. But I can't sustain the illusion; memory falters, the refrain is too repetitive. It's no longer

Mozart, just the restrained tumble of the receding tide. And my tooth aches louder than the sea.

How many days since the storm? Eight days since I commenced plotting the night sky on the beach. I think the storm was three days before that. Even now, so soon after, I can't be sure. The days merge. With no future date to look forward to, no planned event in my calendar to await with any degree of anticipation, the whole concept of time has become unclear. I see now that the passage of time matters only when a known occurrence is to take place, such as the start of a workday or the time to go home, a special weekend planned, a holiday, Christmas time. Because one could identify moments in time by such landmarks there was usually an expectancy about the passing of the hours or days or weeks, or whatever unit filled the span. But it was something awaited with a degree of emotion, hope, joy, trepidation or anxiety, so that the careful recording of timeflow was an essential adjunct to the emotional intensity. Even the minor notches of the daily routine depended upon this timeflow record, from some trivial ritual of the day to a crucial appointment affecting one's destiny; the date and the time of day, such vital information, the very basis of history. For me, here in a limbo of timelessness, there is no record, no dates. Though I have created one point, one deliberate point in eternity, a point without meaning to anyone but me, and yet, whatever the reason, a day to anticipate. Twenty days from now I shall again plot the stars. The project is a contrivance, as my chess game is a contrivance, but both are more essential to my stability than any of the crucial appointments of my past.

My record keeping is of the simplest form, merely stones placed in a line, one for each passing day. But simple as it is, it represents a cerebral act, an act beyond the conceiving or understanding of any animal but man. I am distinguished by that act as a conceptual being. For the most part time must be for me as it is for animals, for dogs sleeping in their chains, cows docile and stupid in the meadows, pigeons dozing on the rooftops. They have no concept of tomorrow, or even of the next hour; even the next few minutes must be a hazy formation in their minds. Do hounds chasing a fox visualise the moment of capture, of the rending and the blood, or do they feel only the moment, the excitement of 'now'? Without the forward projection they must be agitated primarily by instinct and adrenalin, but if one concedes that dogs waiting by their food bowls to be fed must have at least a limited conception of the future, that it is not simply a matter of routine or of habit, then one must also concede that hounds do visualise the capture of a fox, that they are capable of imagination. Still, the span of time seen clearly can only be a trait of man, although squirrels storing nuts for the winter time must be capable of fore-thought, even though they do not record the passing of days with little stones.

'Squirrels are creatures of instinct. As they store their nuts they do not recognise that one day they will eat them.' It was an emphatic statement. Muller wasn't in his nightshirt; he had on a sleeveless grey pullover over a pinstripe shirt, a white shirt with blue stripes and it had no collar. The sleeves were buttoned down with cuff-links and gathered above the elbows with elastic sleevebands. The shirt was tucked scruffily into black and unpressed trousers. He still hadn't shaved, but had replaced his nightcap with a grubby mortarboard. It wasn't at all as I remembered Muller.

'I remember you as always being so immaculate.'

'You see me as you want to see me.'

'You're sure about the squirrels?'

'Man is the only animal with the capacity for rational thought.'

'How can you say that?'

'Do you disagree?'

'Perhaps not, but I question your emphasis.'

'I am emphatic because it is true.' Muller tended to be pedantic, but I recall, too, that his pedantry was less that of faith than of teaching method. But he was worn out. Old and tired and worn out, as were his platitudes. I see that everything about him, the ideas he instilled in me, the ideas I have of him, are questionable now. He is scruffy because I reject his standards. I question his emphasis as I question his interpretation of truth.

'What is truth?' I ask. I am at my school desk. He parades his dais. His thumbs are tucked into his trouser top above his arse. He is the master. His utterances are unquestionable. He is the fount of all knowledge. I watch him, tense with awe and the grappling with wisdom.

He fixes me with his bulging eyes, unsupported eyelids red and gaping below. 'Truth is that which is in accord with known reality.'

'Can you define known reality?'

'Facts. Facts. Facts.'

'Then truth is very limited,' I dared to comment, but I was not then at my desk. I faced him on the beach. He looked afraid.

'What are the limitations of truth?' he whispered, vague then. A wraith.

'Wood comes from trees. That is truth because it's indisputable. Hens lay eggs. That is truth. That is in accord with known reality. Squirrels act entirely out of instinct. That is not necessarily truth. That is a supposition. There is a God. That is a concept. It is certainly not known reality.'

Muller left me then, about an hour ago. I wrestle alone for the struggle is mine. There is nothing Muller can contribute. There are my eight stones in a row. That is my concept and my only truth. Damn my toothache.

✳   ✳   ✳

My chess game continues. The weather appears to be taking a turn for the worse; I hope the wind doesn't blow it about, for it's becoming quite intriguing now. It is necessary to consider each move for many hours. Because so many moves are planned in advance and because I am fully aware of the counter-moves of each side, every permutation has to be thought about over and over again. Every possible move opens up many new possibilities. I am absorbed in it now. The game can only be won if an infallible series of moves can be devised. I have to favour no side, and am careful of that. Having worked out a ploy for one side, I then have to ensure that I work out the best possible counter for the other.

The wind is definitely getting stronger while I sit here. There are clouds in the sky gathering rather quickly. It will be necessary to erect a shelter for the chess game. Already the wind is disturbing the pieces. Memorise the situation on the board. Then gather rocks for the windbreak. It is pleasing to have something to do that can be classed as urgent. Any motivation to act is exciting. Even while the wind gusts, I'm savouring my emotional and physical responses to the situation, like the savouring of an unknown wine. I am so aware of everything about myself, every reaction instinctive or conscious, that my awareness is almost clinical. But what else do I have to be conscious of?

*   *   *

This morning is flat. The clouds and the wind were forerunnsrs of nothing. It is a blue morning. I played chess all night and made only two moves. I am irritated by it. I write to soothe the irritation, with the realisation that the annoyance is as much from my blasted toothache as from dissatisfaction with the chess game, but if I concentrate on words, that helps to restore my equilibrium. It is vital to maintain a constancy of perspective so that despair and loneliness won't overwhelm me. The irritation is a trap. I dwell on an emotional surface that must be planular, but with the awareness of quicksands in the plane, the soft clinging muds, the tempting morbid wallows that could smother me.

So it is flat today. A planular surface. There is no danger of becoming morbid, is there? I long desperately for a woman this morning. It's only a physical thing. I want the deep carnal recesses of woman, and it's a need for which there's no satisfactory alternative. It's often with me, of course, this need, and though it is especially intense today, I know it will fade. It will never go entirely. The need lurks there always, disturbing and shaping my dreams, one of the root causes of my shuttered despair, and also of the more tightly shuttered hope.

I am sitting under the palm trees and the view is framed by two wrinkled trunks like the frame of a postcard scene. White sand. Glass-flat sea. Horizon clean and sharp where the shades of blue diverge. The reefs clearly seen beneath an undisturbed surface. A view of paradise. A travel poster.

There is the quicksand. I am closer to it than I will permit myself to accept. I suppose I always am. The words 'damn this place' shudder through me so that I almost call them out aloud, and although there is none to hear and none to comment, I don't allow them to become articulate. Why do I exercise control? Do I fear that the liberation will be a step towards madness? Perhaps the control itself is a symptom of insanity. This morning is bad. A monotone day. A dangerous time. I should do something. I must not just sit here and smother in the mud. I shall swim out to Reef Four.

The reef was especially clear and beautiful, like the first time I visited it. My enjoyment was marred, though, because of this pounding toothache. I am sure there is something rotten in my mouth. The pain dominates me. I swam for a very short time and then ceded to the demands of screeching nerves. I am close to despair this time. I recognise it but don't know what to do. The tooth has to come out. It has to come out.

*   *   *

Of one thing I am absolutely certain: it is not possible for a man to remove one of his own teeth, especially not a back one. The pain goes on. I can do nothing. My control is slipping.

*   *   *

I think it is an infection. My mouth is tender to touch. I shall die now. I shall die of blasted toothache.

That is inconceivable. I will not let it happen. But I can't eat.

I tremble. It is not from fear, nor from cold for it is still very warm. It has to be the infection. I'm ill. I must be ill.

*   *   *

My dreams were black. Time has passed and yet it is the same. How many days? I am very dry and I am very weak. But it has gone. The pain has gone. The sweating and the shuddering have gone. I must have struck my head for there's a swelling and some dried blood on the back of it. I just remember the awful hours, the awful hours of illness and wanting to die. The awful hours of reeling mind and reeling stomach, an empty lurching stomach, an empty lurching skull. The sweat, and the shaking, and sand on my skin. There were moments of clarity, at night. I watched a full moon, wobbling and swinging, bouncing in the blackness. My head throbbed and I stared at the unstable moon. A time of no moon. Of a single star. A single light piercing my brain. Glowing. Growing. Getting bigger and bigger. The light expanded inside my head, swelling my skull. There was unbearable pain. Then times of blackness. There was singing. I remember the singing. I detached. There was an instant when I left my twitching shell. I must have been near death then. But now it's over. It was my ordeal and it's over.

I have drunk but I'm still dry. I might have been days out there in the sun. I see that my chess game is wrecked; kicked to pieces in some unremembered thrashing. I'll have to start all over again; goodness knows how the pieces were situated before, though I should be able to recall it. No matter, I'll start afresh. My record of time will now be inaccurate. That doesn't really matter, either. Does anything matter? I live still, and I want to regret it. I want to regret being alive. Yet what I feel is closer to relief; it's a strange, somewhat tortured relief, my body aching still and my muscles disinclined to move. No, it isn't good to be living, now, here, in this circumstance. It

81

would be better to be dead. Still, there is pleasure in being alive, in being lucid still. And I am glad.

'Why shouldn't you be glad? You do not know death. With no experience of it, how can you state boldly that death is better than life?' He sits there, squatting small and broken in his nightshirt.

'Tell me about death.'

His face is old. The skin sags off his cheekbones, dragging his eyelids down. It is skin the colour of cheese, but blotched with large purple blotches. The eyes are wet, defeated, already dead. Again it is not the Muller I had known. 'I can't tell you about death. You can only experience death. Beyond death there is no other experience.'

'Is there no after-life, then? No heaven at all? No hell?'

'Heaven and hell are experiences of the living.'

'And limbo?'

'Where are you now? Is it not limbo?'

'But limbo is only a plateau, a stage before heaven.'

'Or hell, perhaps.'

'Yes. Or hell. Is this limbo or hell?'

He looks at me as if from a hell of his own. 'What would release mean to you? Would you return to the world perpetually happy or ceaselessly discontent?' He lisps. He almost slobbers his words from his limp, uncontrolled mouth. But the probing is there as he always probed. It was his technique, then as now.

It must be nearly evening. There is a breeze, just slight, cool and smelling of the reef. 'I'll certainly see the world differently, but I can't judge if that will make for discontent. Indeed, I'm sure there will be moments of happiness. I have never believed in perpetual happiness, so I don't expect it. Happiness is an ephemeral thing, and my experience here cannot change that. Sometimes it lingers, though; often the wash of it is more enduring than the moment, but it is really a thing of moments, isn't it? Perhaps the memory of this limbo, if that is what it is, will heighten those moments for me; perhaps the wash will endure, perhaps even last from moment to moment. I imagine I shall nurse that pleasure with added care; I shall not squander it as I used to, with that deliberate destruction of sentiment that was so much a feature of my youth. That can be said to be a legacy of the limbo, if you like.'

He sits there, watching me, his eyes unblinking and colourless like bottled oysters. Muller is crumbling, disintegrating as I watch. The breeze is very pleasant. 'Can you hear the music?' he says.

And I do hear it. The breeze is carrying a melody, lilting and gentle as my father's voice. 'Will you send the girl?' I ask him.

'She is not in my control. Only you can summon her.'

I am aware of that, of course. The question is an idle one, just a spontaneous reflection of a train of thought stirred by the music. The music is perfectly audible, and quite lovely. I'm very thirsty. I'll go now and drink.

*   *   *

I hear music often. It comes at evening time when the breeze is from the south-east, and it mostly comes that way. Of course it is the memory of melody that I hear, the combination of the sounds of the sea and the wind and my need of it, a subconscious projection that is conscious music. But knowing that, recognising it, doesn't dampen my enjoyment in the slightest. It is a trick of mind for which I am grateful. More, I encourage it by submerging the rational explanation beneath blankets of reluctance. I want the music to be real. And it is real. The human mind has an exceptional capacity to deceive itself. Having evolved rational thought as the superlative trait of all living things, giving man dominance of the world, it seems to have evolved a parallel trait within the conscious mind in the ability to listen to the demands of ancient instincts etched into the human psyche long before the supremacy of logic. That is the section of my own brain that I encourage. How old is the need for music? Who can say? Certainly older than man himself, born in the dregs of age when creatures first left the ocean to slither in the strange world of air, when communication

83

with one's kind relied on sound, and later the ability to distinguish sounds. The birth of music is the call of frogs, the sunset chorus of crickets, it is the unheard sounds of a termite queen. Music excites as a mating call excites; it soothes as the clucking of a mother soothes; it relaxes as the reassurance of a greeting relaxes amid the dark of an aggressive world. The need for music is the need for security, and must be one of the fundamental needs of creatures of the land. So I have created mine and satisfied that need. Or is the satisfaction as much a delusion as the music itself?

I have not written for several days. I have been swimming, but not a great deal, for the illness left me quite weak. I am stronger now. Muller visits me frequently and we have many wide-ranging discussions. I haven't recorded them, but I find that as Muller is an aid to crystallising my thought, so writing it down assists the perspective. As thinking is my prime occupation, I ought to record the process of my reflections, so that when I'm rescued I can reconsider the conclusions of isolation in comparison with the frantic considerations of urban life. The girl came once and I ravished her. What a fantasy! I can't touch her. She is not an embodiment as Muller is. She has to remain ephemeral, the image only of spectral desire.

There was a slight shower of rain and there is fresh water. The chess game is set up once more and a match is nearing finality; white will win unless I can come up with a new stratagem to prevent it. I think about twenty-eight days have passed since the first time I plotted the heavens on the sand. Tonight I'll do it again. My tooth is aching once more, but it is a local pain, just one tooth, not my whole mouth, and I can endure it. I have reconciled myself to having constant pain there, though it does cease hurting quite often and for hours at a time. The relief then is in itself a pleasure.

The illness has shown me the imperative for keeping in good health and condition. I can do no more about my diet than I am doing, but somehow, incredibly, it seems to be adequate. My intake of vegetable food is limited to coconuts, and I haven't had one of those for three weeks; all other sustenance is from the sea and is completely animal in origin. Evidently sea food must contain all the nutrients for good health, for good health and fitness were my only weapons in defeating the infection. I have taken to exercising twice daily, with at least one or two hours of swimming. The exercises consist of push-ups, squats, and running round the island. I doubt if I have ever been so fit, or so strong. I am hard and tough. A real wild man, shaggy, naked, clawed and unashamed. A product of modern education, technological man, cultured, haughty in the arrogance of the social state; trimmed now to claws and teeth, whittled to the gifts of nature, and a penknife. A book, a pencil and a penknife. The residue of technology, and futile in the drive to be. But I mustn't forget the glasses; I'm not totally trimmed to nature's gifts, the glasses have been the essential means of my survival. They give me fire, and they give me conquest of the sea. Who would ever have thought that short-sightedness could be a blessing?

For occupation only I have invented a bird trap. I have no intention of using these rather nasty seabirds for food, but entrapment presents a challenge to my inflated ingenuity. The trap consists of my jacket propped upon a tripod of sticks, with the ribbon made as a fishing line now serving as a string to dislodge the supporting stick should a bird enter the little tent. There is bait inside, the intestines of my latest fish. There are birds around, but so far they are showing a singular lack of interest. I sit under a palm tree holding the end of my ribbon and wait. Waiting I am used to and now it has some purpose, even if I do let my captures go.

It's become quite cold now and my birdtrap has reverted to its designed function as a jacket. I didn't catch a bird. I am clothed as fully as I can be with the remnants of my wardrobe; no longer the naked savage. My trousers are very ragged shorts with a gaping fly; my underpants are unusable as an article of clothing, but my singlet and shirt are relatively undamaged, though heavy with the smell of sweat. The jacket still has two sleeves and covers my trunk but could hardly be recognised as the garment its tailor intended. It's as misshapen and baggy as an old sack and probably less effective, with a vertical tear right down the back plus a button missing and another hanging by a thread; yet three buttons remain to close the front. My socks are equally misshapen. I use them, one over the other, as a balaclava. They keep my head warm and help protect the bad tooth, but the hole made for my face, together with the ever increasing bulk of hair and beard, are causing a rapid disintegration of the socks' unity. They won't last much longer, and I don't know what I can do with the wool.

It is now very dark. The sun has set and so far there is no moon. It won't be long, for the clouds that conceal it are moving rapidly. Stars are being revealed all the time, and some are being engulfed, but I feel the clouds are scurrying too fast to settle in the night sky and soon they will have stampeded into a daylight somewhere. I have been lying on the beach in a quiet enjoyment of the darkness, drinking it, filling my lungs with it, feeling it as I feel the sea when I dive. Spots of stars like scattered salt relieve the envelope of blackness. For some minutes I have felt the contentment of waiting; waiting for the vast revelation of uninterrupted night, waiting to plot it with an eagerness but not an impatience. I have lost the capacity for impatience. It is necessary to peer close to the page to write these words and I've made my eyes ache. But soon my eyes will have to adjust their focus to the ultimate degree, seeing things then that are so far away as to make the vision of them stretch the capabilities of one's mind to understand, things that may not even be there any more.

The light is improving now and I can see the moon, squinting between the racing clouds. Already there are enough stars to begin.

*　　*　　*

The stars have moved amazingly in the twenty-eight days. Admittedly the span of time is uncertain, but it will be close enough for my exercise. It seems that not only does the position of the stars change in relation to the Earth, but their position alters in relation to each other. Indeed, some constellations are to all appearances of fixed shape and dimension – Orion, for example – but constellation to constellation, or constellation to fixed star, appear variable both in distance and position. Question after question arises in my mind as I ponder this discovery, and they fascinate me so much it astounds me that I never bothered to study them before. The most puzzling question is in fact why constellations do retain their constancy; it would seem to incorporate a remarkable combination of coincidences. The answer must be related to distance.

'Muller, why did you not teach me astronomy?' I shout, but Muller doesn't appear.

It has taken me three nights to re-plot the sky on the sand, overlaying my previous exercise to establish the comparison. In order to distinguish the two plottings, I had first to code the original one by ensuring all the shells were of one colour, meaning that more than half had to be changed. There is an abundance of shells on the beach. The new pattern could then be made distinct by the use of another colour, and then next time a third colour, and so on. I don't want to consider the 'so on' too far ahead; I refuse to contemplate beyond the next twenty-eight days. I do enjoy this monthly project; it reflects what is really one of the most important aspects of my solitude, that makes my existence bearable. Occupation. To devise projects, fresh endeavours, that is the key to sanity.

I have this book. I don't bother to read it. I haven't read anything apart from my own writing since arriving here. Yet that one book offers my sole contact with my prior life. I once imagined that life without books would be intolerable; well it is, but not in the same context as the sentiment was considered. It would have been hard then to imagine existence without music or art or poetry. To be utterly barren, to be devoid not only of the products of culture but of all the absorbing gimmickry of the inventive world, aspects of industrial living that fill so many of one's leisure hours – this is the torment of idleness.

I can't garden here, mow a lawn, repair an engine, send a

letter; I can't romp with a dog, I can't do a crossword puzzle. There's only my mind, my convoluted, unclear mind, muddled with the dogma of upbringing, trying to extract truth and clarity from the biased fog; and the philosophies that result, the primitive, introspective philosophies that emanate only because of this predicament, are the products of that dogma and my own meditations. I suppose they must of necessity be introspective with no foil other than the wraiths of my own imaginings. But imagination and reality aren't easily divorced, even in the social state. Muller is real, more real than Deirdre. The music I hear is real. So what is reality? What I feel is reality, yet I must recognise that as distinct from truth.

✳   ✳   ✳

I have succeeded in raising an edifice of sorts. It consists of two parallel walls of stone almost three feet high and somewhat longer, and about that distance apart. Using three boughs from the odd tree to bridge the span, I have roofed it with the turtle shell and what palm fronds I have. It is primitive and too cramped to be adequate, but it's a beginning. It can be improved as more stones are discovered. Already the island has been stripped and it was necessary to wade out to waist depth to find enough suitable rocks even for so small an edifice. Each rock had to be worn by rubbing to allow the one above a stable seating. It has been slow, tedious work, and a task that for the first time on the island prompted an idleness in me, a disinclination to work. But I kept at it, and now I have a shelter. The turtle shell was a sacrifice because it's the best of my reservoirs, but cutting off the boughs from the odd tree was more personally hurtful. The decision to do so was a long time in coming and now it's done I regret it. That tree struggled so hard; it endured the searing sun, it endured the shredding wind, it endured and writhed and grew. It is a metaphor of my own soul. Now I've crippled it, torn the very limbs from it, and I can only pray that I haven't dealt it a mortal blow. The tree is tough, it has proved that; it must recover.

I have been mistaken all this time: there is another creature that shares this island with me other than the crabs on the beach. Today there has been a small, wondrous delight. I held in my hands the most delicate spider I have ever seen, a tiny thing, no bigger than my fingernail with a body hardly the size of an apple seed. It is rounder than an apple seed and coloured with yellow and brown dots; its legs, too, are bands of yellow and brown, but the bands are so fine on the slender legs that it hurts my eyes squinting to distinguish them. It is a miracle, this little spider. I have searched but have found no other. If there is no other, then how did this one happen to be here? Is it possible that it was brought by birds? I wonder if this lovely, fragile fragment of life is the last survivor of a colony whose origins lie with the origins of the grove itself. Has it eaten all its kind? What else could it eat? There are no insects here. The spider lies quiet in my hand, so beautiful and so dainty that I find it hard to visualise it as a fratricidal cannibal. It is so little. Possibly its sustenance is so very minute that my eyes can't see it, motes of living matter carried on the wind. It is all related to the concept of scale. Why else would the spider build a web?

It was the web that revealed its presence, for I could never have spotted it, coloured as it is, against the tones of the branches. I saw the web first when I awoke this afternoon. The day was sultry and, with the sun high, the shelter gave the most shade. Quite an unpleasant day, actually, not one for great activity. I was lying on my back and just above me were the boughs I had cut for the roof. The web was tucked almost out of sight between one bough and a palm frond just above it, looking white and frail in the shadows as if cringing out of sight; so insignificant that I might not have noticed it at all had not the spider chosen that moment to move across it as if adding another thread. For a while I simply looked at it. I seemed at first to feel nothing. Then the questions began to come. And the wonder.

Those to whom a spider on a tree is commonplace, too

ordinary for comment – and indeed I was certainly one of them – would not understand my emotions following the discovery. Yet it was like finding a flower in the desert, or a brilliant gem in the gravel of a river bed. Following the initial movement that betrayed it, the spider did not move again. I lay and watched it for a long time. At last I reached up and brushed it into my hand, and held it. As I gazed at it I felt so strange; it was an affinity with this tiny arachnid, almost an affection. The moment is still vivid. I felt as if I had received an unexpected gift from a loved one, but more than that, for there was a touch of awe about it as if I held something inestimably precious. I talked to it in the unnatural speech one uses with babies. And I took it into the light and studied it. It remained still, showing not the least sign of distress.

Later, with the utmost care, I replaced it in the web. Then I searched for others, looking for the webs rather than the virtually invisible creatures themselves. I find myself repeatedly checking to see if my spider is still there, but in fact it hasn't moved.

It is now sunset and it's cooler. I hope the humidity presages rain.

*   *   *

I've caught another turtle, bigger than the previous one. Its carapace will be most useful for my roof. I caught it in the sea. I was swimming in the shallows, already coming ashore with a lobster, when there was the turtle crossing in front of my nose, placid, making no attempt to increase its pace. I simply dropped the lobster and grabbed it. It jerked strongly then, but I was able to stand up, lifting it from the water, and to wade ashore, clutching it to my chest.

There isn't much fuel left, but I intend to use the rest tonight. I'll have turtle soup, and then turtle steak. It feels like Christmas Day. It could very well be, I suppose. Tonight I shall celebrate; I'll sing Christmas carols; Deirdre will come and dance; there will be wine and women and song. It will be a feast.

Yuletide. Ah, there are so many memories stored of this ancient feast. I remember our kitchen. There was holly there, and mistletoe, of course, weird druidical symbols whose significance is buried beneath the layers of the educational revolution – sadly, for there is still a magic in the decorations of nature that one doesn't feel with paper chains. But we had paper chains, too, homemade and of the most random design and colours. It was fun making the paper chains, a part of the anticipation of Christmas that I remember most happily. There was my mother in the kitchen – it was always in the kitchen – cutting up bits of coloured paper that she had put aside during the whole year for the occasion, while her three children squabbled over the paste pot. I call to mind being happily covered in paste; it was on my face and the taste of it in my mouth. That happened every year, I suppose, but my recollection records me as being about ten years old. That must have been the first year that memories were filed away with any clarity; the younger years faded quickly, I imagine, and became merged into that one. But perhaps it was just an especially memorable year.

It seems now, looking back, that it was the anticipation of the great day that was the best time of all. As I remember it all, I find that I'm filling up with nostalgia. I let it come, the feelings of sadness and joy and gratefulness that it happened. The memories flow and I abandon myself to them. The anticipation was the best, but Christmas Day was never an anticlimax. Even so, not one gift received stands out as particularly special. I know that I received many over the years. There were jigsaw puzzles. I see myself on the floor, not far from the stove, mother stepping over me repeatedly, carefully but with muted grumbles. She never made me move. That was Christmas Day: I did jigsaw puzzles. That cameo of recollection encompasses the whole day. But there was food, a supply line of food coming inexhaustibly from that great cast-iron range. Mother smiling through her toil – she smiled much on Christmas Day. Father happy, always home for the great day. Children everywhere; on his legs, on his lap, on his back. Toys scattered over the floor. The memories cascade. Misty pictures, perhaps not as it was, perhaps composites of many times, snapshots of Yuletide scenes, perhaps blended in memory with scenes read and scenes portrayed on postcards, or of how one wished it was. But it's near to the truth. Christmas Days were most happy times.

There is one fact that I recall, although it's hardly of any significance, and that is that we never had a tree. The kitchen was too cluttered for a tree. We lived in that kitchen. There was only the kitchen and the bedrooms and a small bathroom outside that was always full of washing. There is the picture of our dirty clothes piled in a large enamelled bowl placed for that purpose in one corner beside the copper, and all around the room clean clothes hanging from low-strung lines, because my mother was so short. One was forever evading washing in the bathroom. We bathed in an enamel tub that had to be filled and emptied by hand and which had an irremovable grey line at navel height when sitting in it; a line that completely encircled the bath, but indistinct, fixed there forever by years of holding exactly six buckets of water from the copper, varying only in height by the size of the body immersed in it.

But the kitchen was the focus of our home, and the focus of the kitchen was the table. It was a large rectangular monster of a thing, a pale timber colour made even paler by repeated scrubbings. There were eight chairs, all of which seemed to be used, although there were only five in the family. These chairs were large, too, also timber but less pale, for they retained elements of old varnish except on the seats which were quite grey from our dirty trousers. Behind the table, across the room from the stove, stood an enormous dresser. All our furniture was of the large sort. I recall the dresser having gaping joints as if it was about to fall apart. It was ornate and massive and composed of an intricate series of drawers and doors, with shelves and carved fretwork above. Below the shelves – all of them – were hooks from which dangled an amazing assort-ment of cups, never more than two of a set, most of them cracked but kept glisteningly clean. The shelves were piled high with crockery of all shapes and sizes, so that they could only remain fixed by sheer defiance of all laws of structural capacity. Yet fixed they remained, and remain so still, so far as I know.

The kitchen had two doors: one beside the dresser, which led onto a passage and thus to the staircase giving access to the bedrooms, and behind the staircase to the front door and a storage cupboard under the stairs. We had no other downstairs rooms. There was another door in the kitchen beside the stove and to the left of the sink. It was a china sink, once white, but even in my childhood it was the colour of old straw, with thousands of fine cracks, like spiders' webs, in the glaze. There was a single cold water tap to service it and all the plumbing was exposed.

There was no other furniture in the kitchen, only a continuous narrow shelf, at doorhead height, completely encircling the room. Upon this shelf was a motley assortment of ornaments, books, vases without flowers, bits of paper and photographs in frames. Many had remained unmoved for years and were thick with grease and dust, because mother, who was scrupulously clean where she could reach, never cleaned above the reach of her arms. There was one photograph almost above the stove which was so covered with grime that it wasn't possible to see the portrait behind the glass. I remember once, as a child, climbing onto a chair and, by stretching from tip-toe, managing to get it down. Behind the glass were the faded, smiling features of a young man rigid in uniform. I couldn't identify the uniform, or the young man. Mother washed off the grease and replaced the picture on the shelf. It was grimed again within six months and probably hasn't been touched since. She never informed me of the man's identity, but perhaps I didn't ask.

It is strange how long-forgotten details of my childhood suddenly assume shape and movement in my mind, sharp images like peep shows at an amusement park. I have never given thought to the incident of that photograph since the moment it was replaced, yet now the scene is vivid in recollection. I have indulged nostalgia now beyond its ability to affect me, but the writing down of the memories has been like a re-experience of the past. I have felt it, perhaps but a filtered shadow of what I felt at the time; yet where new experiences are as limited as here, then reliving old ones must serve as a substitute. I must cultivate my facility for recall; there is a storehouse to tap within my mind if I can learn the key to unlock it.

But now I must light a fire and cook a turtle.

✳   ✳   ✳

It hasn't rained now for two weeks. There is no fresh water and still no coconuts, so I have to resort to drinking from the brackish soak. The tides are higher than normal because the moon is fat and close, and the island shrinks accordingly. There has been a lot of wind lately and it gets very cold. But no rain. The sea is choppy and there are strong currents off the shallows which prevent me from visiting Reef Four. The boredom is overwhelming. I play chess but am already starting to cheat with myself, which is plainly absurd. There are other games that I've devised, physical games involving bowling empty coconut shells or throwing stones at designated objects, such as a wicket of sticks or a hole in the sand. There is a variety of these games but they are basically similar and soon become tedious. They are games of accuracy and timing and, without competition to make them relevant, there is no measure of merit or stimulus for improvement. I have considered unravelling the wool in my socks and reknitting an improved balaclava. Although I don't know the skills of knitting, it has always seemed a simple enough technique, and the manufacture of two needles would present few problems. There is in me a streak of what can only be described as pig-headedness, for even now, I balk at the idea of doing women's work; but it is only a mental balking emanating from the falsity of male ego, and I shall most certainly make an attempt to knit, even if the attempt is a form of self-justification. There would be an irony in believing that a woman might possess a skill making her more fit to survive alone on an island than I am. It is an exaggerated concept, of course; many men knit, and not all women. Martine certainly didn't, and I can't recall that Monique did, either.

But would a woman survive as I have survived in the same circumstances? My instinctive reaction to such a question is almost scornfully negative, but what assets do I have that a woman doesn't have? Well, there are the dubious benefits of muscular superiority, and in some instances that is an equally spurious claim. What is more, that asset hasn't really been a factor in my survival. I swim and dive well, and that was always a talent, but I've known several young women who surpassed me in those activities. No, upon reflection, the only time when physical strength might have been an asset was in climbing a coconut tree, but if I had conceived the idea of a peg ladder earlier, that wouldn't have been necessary. I suppose a woman could not have carried the heavier rocks up from the sea bed, or caught a turtle in the sea as I did, but neither factor would have meant non-survival.

Yet could a woman have accepted the mental agony of aloneness, could she have coped with this aspect as I have done? In that, I think, lies the essential difference. Companionship means so much more to a woman than to a man. I believe a woman would have surrendered very quickly to the spectres of despair, for a woman's soul is attuned to responding, to heeding the needs of others – whether her children or her men – and this is a facet of her being that is engraved into her very genes, much as some may deny it; it is a vital factor in a woman's well-being. Without it, solitude becomes more than loneliness as the reason for her existence is erased. Or is that my male ego directing my opinion? Perhaps I do malign the female sex. It is conceivable that women have a greater capacity for loneliness than men, perhaps even a greater capacity for survival. Local knowledge would be the most beneficial asset, knowledge of the possibilities of coconut palms, sea shells, fish bones; such knowledge is not the exclusive province of gender. The other major requirement is that of short-sightedness.

Still, I don't accept it. I don't accept that a woman could stand the loneliness and the rigours of my life here. It may be a fallacy or an opinion born of ego, but this is *my* experience, and that gives no other person the qualifications to debate it. In this, my word has to be final. Indeed, in such dialectic my word is the only one. Even Muller has nothing to say, and as for Deirdre, she has no substance.

I talk to my spider. I hold him in my hand and don't feel him. I am unaware of him having eaten anything since I found him, and he rarely moves. There are times when I think he must be dead, especially when he sits so still in my hand. But he lives. If I stir him with a finger he will deign to shift a leg in irritation, but he makes no move to run. I have developed a tremendous and somewhat maudlin affection for him. But I don't hold him often; I am so conscious of his fragility.

✻   ✻   ✻

The cold continues. The wind continues. My brain is playing tricks. I write to relieve my utter tedium. This pencil is short now and writing is not easy, but neither is my mind always lucid. I lose hours again. Lethargic hours, semi-comatose, unthinking, stupefied. And what scares me even more are the lurid hours. People come. I dance and run shrieking about the beach, lusty and carnal like a crazed Pan. I fear that madness is already perched on my shoulder. The music comes in wild crescendos as if a demented orchestra played beyond the horizon, with clashing cymbals and pounding drums, and then gentle as a choir of children. Even now, with my mind stable again, I hear it; not demonic while sanity prevails, but sweet music reaching me like a sonic caress. I can almost believe an orchestra does play there.

I swam today. I made an effort to get to Reef Four, but the current was very strong and I ceded to caution. It isn't pleasant swimming in choppy water with a mask on. I didn't get a fish or a lobster so it's abalone for dinner. Raw abalone; there is no fuel for a fire.

Why don't I give up? What does it matter if there's a current off the beach? If I get swept out to sea and drown, won't that be better than this present misery with looming madness? There can't be any value whatever placed on this wretched existence. I live. That is all. I continue to breathe and sleep and eat and urinate, and occasionally to think. I don't belong here, as the odd tree doesn't belong here. I am alien to this place. It is alien to me. I am just defiling it, but equally it is defiling me. It is destroying any vestige of soul that I have salvaged from my vicissitudes. It is destroying my mind.

'It is not the island that is defiling you, only your circum-stances.'

It isn't Muller this time. It is someone else. I have created another wraith. A wraith of hair and beard and a misshapen jacket. It is a demon. It is me. I am my own demon. But he is not as I am; he is taller, finely built, confident.

'What is the difference? The island is my circumstance, isn't it?'

'The island was here before you and it will be here long after you have gone. You may be a circumstance to it, but it is not a circumstance to you.' He is smiling. Arrogant sod!

'Then we are a mutual circumstance,' I say.

'The island is indifferent to you. It exists and is content to exist. It is an island. It is content to be an island. It doesn't want to be a mountain; it doesn't want to be a continent. In time it may become either of these things, but in time so immeasurable that the future, like the past, is beyond consideration. The island is happy as it is in time, and your instant upon it means no more to it than the shadow of a cloud.'

'Then it is different from me because I do see the past, even if I see little for my future.' He seems to be bigger, growing like a genie from a bottle. I shout up at him: 'I am as indifferent to the island's being as it is indifferent to mine.'

'You have too much vanity,' he crows, strutting before me. He's very tall, very strong, supreme in his dominance. I am looking up higher and higher. The head is vague above me, a large hairy object with the features tangled and indistinct. 'You need the island, but it doesn't need you.'

He is gone. He was not a true wraith. He wasn't created from my subconscious mind, rather a conscious projection. An *alter ego*, but a pretender. He was false. I am not arrogant within, though sometimes I act so. I am not vain, not inside; I quiver there. I whimper. I feel only contempt for my spineless soul.

I will reach Reef Four. Today. The past days of inaction and idle fantasies, of hovering insanity, of introverted deceit, have decided me. I won't allow the spectres to conquer. Idleness is their ally. But the sea is still choppy, perhaps less so than yesterday but not pleasant. Yet the clouds are scattered and high. The sky is quite blue. The water should be clear and the tide is coming in now; there is less current on the rising tide.

*   *   *

I should not have done it. It was folly; sheer, inexcusable folly. I am back and alive, and very clear about my relationship to the island. I love it. I lay on the beach when I finally attained it and I adored it. I clutched it fiercely. It was an embrace, I wanted to imprint myself into its very rock. This is my island, my haven, my sanctuary. Island, I'm not indifferent to you. I love you. You are my life and I want to live. Astonishingly, I want to live.

I thought that the current was not too strong. Indeed I made it to Reef Four, although it was a hard swim and by the time I arrived there I ached and felt breathless. It was calmer over the reef, but the current still pulled, urging me ever deeper. It was a combat, not too difficult at first; I could swim against it without too much trouble. I drifted to start with, resting from my swim and enjoying the reef. I drifted across it and swam back, and drifted again. That was quite easy. But imperceptibly the return against the current began to require more and more effort, until I was actually swimming really hard to cross it. As the current grew stronger I was growing increasingly tired, and my muscles were beginning to protest. At this stage I was still confident and felt no alarm; protesting muscles were not the forerunners of collapse, and I had faith in my fitness. It was not until the moment when I appeared to be swimming without making any progress at all that the first tremors of alarm ran through me. Even then it only took increased effort to produce forward movement. I began to relax again, and then I began to lose ground. It was difficult to quell the automatic panic that welled up. Again I forced more effort into my stroke and again recovered ground, but I knew that I couldn't maintain that degree of power for very long. It was time to head for shore.

It was then that I realised the waves were much bigger than on the outward trip. The wind had come up. Soon it began to rain. My mask kept filling and I couldn't afford to tread water to empty it. Each time I tried I lost several yards. Finally I took it off and fastened the belt around my waist. It was one article I was not going to risk losing.

Immediately I lost my bearings. I knew the sea floor well but without the mask I couldn't see it. Neither could I see the shore above the waves. The island might not have existed. I was a piece of flotsam in a great expanse of ocean. I don't recall feeling that way when I first swam to the place from the plane. I don't recall fighting a current. The sea was calm on that day and I remember seeing the palms like an arm beckoning. It was a hard swim – I remember that – fully clothed and in a state of shock, but it was nothing to the ordeal I was about to face.

Where was the island? Were the waves heading straight for shore? With such a chop it was hard to establish their basic direction. But the current was parallel to the shore. Swim directly across it. Swim across the current. Keep swimming. Don't slacken. It requires more effort over the sand than over the reef; that's where the current was strongest. Maintain the rhythm. Keep moving. Don't tread water. Don't look up.

But I knew my arms were moving more slowly. They felt like limp sleeves, without power or resilience. My breathing was too rapid, it was a gasping and gulping, and fear was a pain in my throat. It was more and more of a struggle just to keep my head above water. I was swimming more vertically than horizontally. I knew that I couldn't make it. I could no longer recognise the current. Direction had completely deserted me. There was no strength left, no direction and no determination.

I would not die. I didn't think of death at all, in fact. I simply kept my head up. There was no other purpose in me. I can't recall any thoughts at all. I just remember the agony of the struggle to maintain breath. I remember choking and swallowing water. Often. That was my pain and my panic. That was my horror. I kept my head up, not always out of water. Hour after hour. Why? Why didn't I just let go and drown? I can't answer that. I don't know. I don't think it occurred to me. It was such a terror, such an instinctive and all-encompassing terror to swallow water that I could not have allowed it to happen as a deliberate act. I know now that I shall never swim away in a purposeful act of achieving death. Terror is an acid that has etched a deep and horrifying scour on my mind. To drown is that terror. To breathe water is that terror.

My feet touched bottom. They were feet without life and they must have touched the bottom long before the realisation of it. I walked out to the shallows. Somehow. On legs that wouldn't respond. A few yards only. I crawled then. And finally I lay on the sand and felt the swollen wash of gratitude, and felt the love. It was still day. Perhaps only six hours since I had left the beach. I had landed on the western-most point of the island. The current apparently sweeps into shore at that end.

It is the following day now and I still ache. All my muscles seem to ache. Fortunately my tooth is giving me a respite. But I'd rather ache than be dead. Now I know something of death, I'll never think as casually about it as has been my habit of late. Now I know with all certainty that I don't want to die, not by drowning, at least. No matter how wretched my existence I shall preserve it. Life, my life, has value. Without it I am less than a blade of grass, not even a fragment, not the smallest speck of recorded history other than this pitiful pencilling in this pitiful book. Not even my death would be recorded, only my birth in some parochial archive. There is the sum total of my mark on the world: my date of birth, registered and forgotten. In the other world out there, that still churns and swirls like some endless clockwork, in that world I would at least be mourned; there would be someone to grieve my passing. Do people mourn me now? Have I been recorded as simply 'missing, whereabouts unknown', or perhaps 'presumed dead', or is even that just a vanity? Has any word been written of my absence at all? Possibly my disappearance hasn't been noticed. People who know me might still be awaiting my return, merely slightly puzzled by the length of my absence but with faith that I shall come back, one day.

Did I have any importance at all in that world? Oh, some few people had a regard for me, I think, and one or two would have loved me, but they will not be hurt for they can't know of my straits, and if I never return the passage of time will already have grown new skin over what might have been pain. Though there were things that mattered, too, not only people. What of the imperatives that drove me? What of the causes that I believed in? They will not falter one small step for my lack of presence. I must have deemed myself of some value to something, but even that molecule of self-esteem I see now as an exaggeration. I have no value in a world of uncounted millions. I leave no void. One man is an utterly dispensable creature. My endeavours, my urgencies, my posturings, once so intense in their mattering, so dramatic in their meaning to me, are seen now to have been worthless illusions in the grinding on of society. Yet when I return to that society, when I pick up the threads of living again, shall I still be urged by the same imperatives? Will the drives of right and wrong, of justice and injustice, be as clear to me as they appeared before? Or will this aberration of solitude have created a concept of worthlessness that will affect my actions forever?

'Do not lose faith in yourself.'

'It's not a matter of faith, old man. It's a matter of appreciating one's scale in the vastness that is life.'

'We all have a place.'

'Oh, go away.' I don't want his platitudes just now.

*   *   *

The aftermath of my ordeal is with me still, not only the physical weariness but the impact on my attitude. The instinct of self-preservation is so much more than the belaboured phrase spoken by people who know nothing of it, whose opinion is based on the observation of pets and babies. I have learned what it is. It is a living, vibrant force. It is composed of terror and strength and will and defiance. But mainly it is composed of terror. People are afraid to die. All people are afraid to die. All creatures are afraid to die. Consider that. Consider the inbuilt concept of death in all living creatures that makes them so afraid of it. What is so fearful about dying? Is there some record in our genetic pattern that holds an ancient memory of being rent to death by some other voracious organism? Is there a memory of frightful pain associated with the act of dying? Is there a pain that comes with the severance of life?

'It is the dominance of the life force,' says Muller, fully robed in mortarboard and gown. A breeze is blowing but his gown is undisturbed. It is new, black and crisp, marred only by some dandruff and loose hairs on the shoulders.

'What is?'

'The instinct of self-preservation. The life force is so strong it refuses to surrender. It isn't terror. It isn't some inbuilt fear of the moment of death.'

'I know what it is, old man. It is terror, and it is the terror that makes one fight.'

'Terror is of the mind,' he says glibly, 'it has nothing to do with instinct.'

'Well then, let us not call it instinct.'

He is very smart today. He droops a little, but one remembers that he is older than his death. He hasn't shaved, though. I see now that he hasn't shaved. 'Consider life,' he raps, his arms tucked in the flow of his new gown, indisputably

102

the master, 'it is a miracle of evolution. A chemical improbability beyond all calculable odds, and more than that, more than chemistry. If the first speck of life had not possessed a most powerful determination to be, it would not have been. That is how old the instinct of self-preservation must be. It is the primal heritage.'

He parades the beach as he once did his dais. But he never taught us such things. He taught us the theory of Pythagoras. He taught us the Principle of Archimedes. They were demonstrable. They were facts.

'That's a beautiful theory, old man. I like it.'

'It's preferable to your theory of terror,' he says. But he won't look at me. He won't show me his face of stubble and floating eyes. Already the weight of his new gown is bearing him down.

'But isn't it the same thing? Your primal heritage is the fear of non-existence. It is terror, the terror of oblivion.'

'No, no. It is the obverse of fear. It is the striving to be. It is the seed of courage, the seed of achievement. It is the seed of the soul and, as man is infinitely more complex than the first speck of life, so the soul that he has is more complex than its seed. And because life is not only complex but of endless variety, so souls are of infinite variety.'

'Then all living things have souls. Cabbages, mushrooms, even seaweed.'

'Of course.' He certainly never taught us that.

'And because this essence of the soul is the drive to live, when death comes, the soul must also die.'

He is quiet. The wind is tugging at him. He is small and pathetic. His gown seems greyer now and is already torn at the hem. He crumples within it. He says: 'The works of man live on after him.' The phrase is exactly as he used to say it. The concept of primal heritage has already dropped into the worn rut of platitude. 'Works are made of the mind and the hand and the soul. So souls live on.'

I won't accept that homily. I say: 'It's a pretty sentiment but it evades the issue, old man. It is a trick to pre-empt further

103

exploration of the whole substance of your original theme.'

'It's a matter of interpretation, isn't it? If we are to discuss the soul, we must first define the soul.' He is being petulant.

'That quality of an organism that isn't chemical. You have already defined it.'

'What of love? What of sensitivity? What of dreaming?'

'You have reverted to the traditional concept, old man, and it makes me sad.'

'Aren't they facets of the soul, then?'

'Oh yes, parts of the soul, as arms and legs are parts of the body; and as the colour of hair differs in individuals, and the size of breasts differs, so those facets of soul differ. For me, love may not be the same as it is for you. Were you ever in love, Muller?'

He looks at me, mouth gaping, eyes gaping, his old and shabby gown slack about his scrawniness. 'Love,' he mumbles. And then again, 'Love,' and it is a moan of muted anguish.

He is gone. My thoughts have turned from souls to love. 'You didn't come back.' The voice is reproving but tender. Monique is there. Fat Monique with four dimples in her smile. Lust stirs but no memories. 'Why didn't you come back?'

'Did you wait long?' I ask, because I'm struggling to understand. Why, indeed, did I leave her?

'I waited for two years. In a way, I'm still waiting.'

'But there was George, wasn't there?' Something is coming back, but just fragments, like excavating an ancient burial mound. 'You were sleeping with him.'

Her eyes are lovely. She has wonderful eyes. Monique was a gentle, adoring woman, a woman of empathy and immediate responses. She is dressed now in that white pleated dress which was so unsuitable, exaggerating her obesity. I remember her grossness in nudity and the lust becomes a strong physical urgency. She speaks in her soft voice: 'I knew George before you, my love. It would have broken him to leave him. But it was you that I loved.'

How much truth is there in that fabrication? And as I think that, she fades and is gone. I see that one's libido will always weave a fabric of fiction to sustain its vanity. So I shall accept the fabric even if there's more of fantasy than reality within it. I don't want to know the truth, if there is now a truth, for time has already distorted the emotions and motives of the past for all the players in it. Truth is of the instant. Memory of an instant must immediately distort it. So, there is no truth, only near-truths. Truth is a relative concept and must always contain the unspoken definition: truth can only mean something like the truth. I suppose it doesn't matter, really. We tend to base all our actions on what we think is truth, whether our intention is to conceal it or to draw conclusions from it, and for each of us our own version is the measure of our integrity.

My truth is that I'm alone, and I'm tired with a tiredness pervading my very bones. And still I'm thirsty.

*　　*　　*

Today is a clear day. A tranquil time. A good day to visit Reef Four, but I am yet afraid. I have fed my spider with a minute speck of abalone meat, lodging it into the web, but it's still there untouched. It does not appear to have eaten a thing since I discovered it, but I know it's still alive because a small rupture in the web that I caused when placing the crumb of meat there has been repaired. These are the first words I have written for several days. I muse much. There is a contentment in the still hours of the night, and in the evening when the daylight draws on the gown of darkness in a hushed display of petticoats, and prods the waking mind to meditate. Still no rain. My toothache comes and goes; it often goes. I can bear it.

Last night was one of music. All night there was music. I hear it even now. Looking to the south-east from where it comes I can see nothing, but surely it is more than mental trickery. Last night the music was decidedly real. Still it is real. Less pervading without the starlight, but real none the less.

I have climbed one of the coconut trees. There was a compulsion to extend my vision on the conviction that there had to be a source of the music. From the treetop the horizon was as unvaried as from the beach. I strained my eyes. For perhaps an hour I stared. I'm not sure. I did see something. Or thought I saw something. Possibly my mind insisted that I see something. No more than the merest hint of an imperfection on the ruled division between sea and sky. It cannot be. There is nothing there. One's own mind is a practised deceiver.

There are young coconuts on the trees. They give me something to look forward to.

*   *   *

I saw my first shark today. On Reef Four. It cruised placidly enough, showing little interest in me. I remained still, hoping thus to avoid detection, but it seemed to be patrolling a circuit. Unfortunately I was within that circuit, afraid, but not as afraid as I had imagined I would be. The shark was about six feet long, much the same length as me, swimming with idle flicks of its tail. The other fish on the reef were seemingly unalarmed by its presence, although I'm sure they were less active than normal. Eventually, as I grew familiar with the sight of it, my fear abated and I, too, began to swim, but cautiously and straight for shore. As I changed course, the shark veered also. I swam more hurriedly then, looking behind me all the while. I made it to shallow water within minutes, but they were the longest minutes of my life. For the shark followed me all the way in, not aggressively, perhaps just curious. I was not prepared to check its motives.

There is now a new element in the fundamentals of my existence. Swimming for me *is* existence. I have considered the possibility of meeting sharks many times, but without proof of their presence the thought of danger was only a minor factor, too minor to disturb my confidence. It has now assumed the proportions of a major factor, one that I am sure will affect me every time that I enter the water. True, this shark is the only one I have encountered in all the months I have been here, yet now I know without doubt that sharks do inhabit these waters, that must be a constant awareness in my mind. Of course this one may just be a rare visitor, but it might also be taking up residence on my reefs.

I can't bear the thought of always having to keep to the shallow reefs. Even more, the idea of abandoning Reef Four forever fills me with dejection. Perhaps the shark isn't dangerous; after all, they're not all man-eaters. But I'm afraid of it and no amount of rationalisation will defeat such fear. In my predicament it wouldn't be necessary to lose a limb; even to be slightly torn would be a mortal wound. There is no means of staunching blood flow, no means to stitch a tear in my flesh, and not one aid to prevent infection.

I'm calm now, writing of it; my mind is weighing the situation quite coolly. But in truth, it's really like an islet in a swamp; around my thinking mind is a morass of hopelessness. The slimy phantoms of defeat clutch and suck, and my little self-built sanctuary, my weary rock of resolution, is but a temporary defence against them. Sometimes they seem to rise up, to swell and engulf me, and it takes a supreme effort of conscious resistance to sustain the lucid core.

The shark is more than a nuisance. The shark is a calamity. An overwhelming calamity. If I can't swim I must die. I shall die of hunger, or I shall die of laceration. I shall bleed, and I shall bleed, and I shall bleed. God help me! The picture is vivid before me. It is the phantoms, I know it is the phantoms. I can't beat them. My brain is whirling now. Where is my control? Write it down, put it into words, be rational. It is the despair now, the oh so familiar despair. It is beating me. I can't hold it at bay.

※　　※　　※

There's plenty of fresh water, but I'm hungry. I've eaten a few abalone and some crabs. Fear still prevents me from fishing, and even the lobsters in the shallower waters are wary these days, and readily evade me. Two days have passed since I saw the shark and the utter hopelessness has left me, but the fear remains, less graphic now but no less tenacious after hours of deliberating. The shark occupies all my thoughts. I can't dismiss it. The shark is in my spirit and will not be eradicated. I'll have to face it. Of course I'll have to face it. I must swim out to Reef Four and be with it. But the courage will not come, despite my mental belabouring; I dither here, knowing my own dispirit, struggling for some degree of resolution. I remember my months of arrogance; I was the king, I had conquered my environment. Ah, but it was easy to be arrogant when fears were inanimate, when the only dangers were my mind, my health or the forces of nature. Now the menace is another form of animate life, a distinctly aggressive form of life, a creature superbly equipped for aggression and one with a reputation for exactly that. And my fear is a new type of fear. A physical, cringing thing. I had a fear of dogs as a boy. It is probably still part of my essential being, and this fear of the shark is of the same kind.

I must have been about three years old, maybe four, when the fear was woven into my soul. There was a narrow lane behind our house, a lane of dislocated paving used only for foot traffic, between the high street and the residential area further back, and also as a playground for the children of our domain. It was probably on my first venture alone along the lane towards the mysterious and fascinating high street that the incident occurred which laid the foundation for my present abjection. The older children would have been at school. I suppose that I was being disobedient, and I suppose there was trepidation, curiosity certainly, and excitement, but those emotions have not survived in memory. Only the dread remains. I don't even recall reaching the high street. I remember the dog. In recall it was huge and black, with massive yellow teeth, but that was the impression of a terrified child and there would be little reality in it. Probably it was just an exuberant young dog wanting to play, reacting to its instinct to chase. I remember it barking and myself running berserk and screaming along the lane. It barked at my heels. I tripped. The barking was all around me, over me, right in my ears. I lay on the ground and shrieked. I was still shrieking when Mother picked me up. I was shrieking even after that. My childhood was imprinted thereby, stamped for all time with an unreasonable dread of all dogs. I was even aware of a submerged fear later on, with a pet of my own. That is the essence of my cowardice.

Yet it is more than that. It is a more primal fear. Part of my soul, part of my heritage. The known and understood fear of dogs, with its known and understood origins, is only part of the total terror. There is an ancestral timidity, more ancient than man himself, born of the lurkings of forebears when trepidation was a virtue, was indeed the vital factor in survival; born from times when imprudence meant a most savage death. And this ancestral timidity was steeped ineradicably into the heritage of man. I don't believe there is such a thing as a fearless man; brave men, yes; men who can conquer the dread, men with a cause and a will beyond all the dictates of heritage; and some men who fall victim to their own bravado, reluctant heroes, as it were. But I am none of these.

Yet I am a rational man. Reason will in time give me control of ancestry. It was quite a small shark, really.

*   *   *

I sit on the beach and stare to the south-east, to that possibility of another place. I know the exact position on the horizon that could be an intrusion on its level perfection, that could be another island, or even the headland of a larger place. I don't see it now, but I have seen it more than once. This morning, when the sky was unmarred by haze or reflections, when the blueness of space was immense flat colour, unchanged in hue or density, like great painted walls of a cavern, and I could see the end of distance, then I saw that intrusion. I know I saw it. It was not imagination. I heard the music and I saw the place. I must have seen the place.

*   *   *

The little spider was gone when I awoke today. I sat for several awful minutes while my soul emptied. It was the same feeling that one experiences when one has learned of a betrayal of trust, the infidelity of a lover or the death of a close friend. Just a blackness at first, a refusal to believe; then a hollowness, a distraction, so that one doesn't even heed one's own thoughts, one doesn't even hear them. To feel in such a way over a spider would seem absurd, but that would be a judgement of an occupied mind and an occupied heart. I felt that way, and it was as much a mental shock as any I've experienced. It lasted for a little while, but soon reason settled sluggishly and I examined the deserted web. It was unbroken still. Had the little fellow died and simply fallen out? There was no trace of him on the floor of the shelter. And then I saw it, a new web in almost the same place on the second bough, practically indistinguishable from the first. And there he sat, calm and patient, while my heart exploded with delight. It seemed to me a most extraordinary thing that, in the space of a few hours, the spider could move without a sign of his passage and spin a new web, and that web would seem to comprise as much bulk as that of the spider. I brushed him into my hand and replaced him on the old web. It didn't appear to disturb him.

I sit outside now and ask: 'Muller, has my spider got a soul?' He doesn't answer so I waft further questions into the emptiness. I talk loudly; he has to hear me and respond. 'If he dies, does his soul die, too?'

'You must draw your own conclusions,' he says. It is just his voice. A calm, reasoned voice. There is mastery in it still. 'I am merely the other side of your chess game. You always play alone.'

'I know that, damn you. Appear. I'm not going to talk to a voice.'

'I am here.' He has come at my bidding like a genie. He sits beside me in his nightshirt. He looks frail.

'Are you a soul?' I ask.

'You know what I am.'

'Yes. You are death. You're the death of false teaching. You're the death of indoctrinated philosophy.'

110

'No, it must not die. It is composed of the interpretation of certain truths. You may redefine that composition but you cannot abandon the truths within it.'

'Is the idea of the primal heritage truth?'

'It's a concept, isn't it, a way of defining an abstract?'

'Is soul an abstract, then? If that is so, life itself must be abstract, because we have said that life comprises chemistry and soul.'

'Chemistry isn't abstract.'

'But chemistry occurs without life.'

The sun beats down on his wrinkled scalp. It looks yellow and delicate as a dried leaf. The few strands of hair wither in the heat. 'The soul may exist without life, too,' he murmurs, 'but not as ghosts or spirits in the accepted sense. Consider the complexity of the chemistry involved in the most simple living cell, and then consider the primal heritage in the same context. It is an abstract, but it is part of a continuum of natural occurrences, just as chemistry is.'

'So we call it abstract, and life is a combination of that abstract force and the effects of chemistry.' He nods and I wonder if his head will fall off. His eyes slosh about and his jaw has trouble lifting with his head. 'That makes it sound like electricity.'

The sea stretches flat and stubbled like a field newly mown, and in the sunlight it is a sheet of constantly changing glints. The water will be clear, but the broken surface makes the reefs invisible from where we sit. I am in the shade, but beside me Muller is in the direct sun. 'Move over to this side,' I suggest, and he does so. He has managed to get his jaws together and he is keeping them clamped tight, the crease of his lipless mouth bent down at the ends, emphasising the thin band of bone beneath. 'Electricity is a physical force,' I go on, 'and must be harnessed according to the laws of physics, and chemical behaviour must also follow the laws of chemistry; similarly with biological behaviour. These laws are well known, they are natural laws which man has discovered and defined. Tell me, old man, what laws does the soul obey?'

111

'All of those and others which still await definition; but, defined or undefined, the soul behaves within certain parameters.'

Now I don't know who is speaking. Am I talking to the old man, or just thinking these words? He is less of an embodiment now. Really just a mental blackboard on which ideas can be chalked and quickly erased. He can be clever, stupid, obtuse or pedantic, just as I wish to see him. He is a most useful fellow.

'Life is the biological force.' These are thoughts. Muller is sitting quite grim and composed beside me still. 'Electricity is a physical force. Radio-activity is, presumably, a chemical force. All the sciences have a related force and life is one of them.'

'Are you trying to explain primal heritage and the soul in the terms of known science?' Muller interrupts.

'I suppose I am. I'm endeavouring to define the parameters of the soul within the confines of the total spectrum. I'm afraid it remains an abstraction. Science should pay more attention to the soul.'

'Religion is concerned with the soul, and there is much religion. Probably more priests than scientists.'

'You are right. But the soul is not the prevail of priests in the context of the force of life. Religion is the preserve of beliefs, and beliefs are of the mind. Mind is but an evolved facet of the soul.'

I write this down as my mind paddles away like a wooden spoon in a bowl of dough. Already the sun has begun its downhill roll and the shadows are missing me. I record it as conversation, although that is not altogether true. The dough stirs sluggishly. 'Once there was a force, a spirit if you like, that combined with a complex molecule to make a living thing. Give that event a religious connotation if you will. But whatever connotation is applied to it, that is what we must comprehend to understand soul. So call it the primal heritage; it's as good a term as any, for it gave all living things the primal drive, the urge to be. Without it there was only chemical activity, relying entirely upon the interrelation of elements. Suddenly there was a consciousness of self that was a determination of

112

identity – in other words, the instinct of self-preservation. In that vital instant was born the will to be, but also selfishness, egotism, arrogance, cruelty – all the facets of that will to be. Of course, that factor alone isn't life: the molecule was the substance of life, the body; the primal heritage was the spirit, just a raw, unevolved cell at that time. It did not endow the organic matter with religion, music, love, dreams or philosophy; all it gave was the determination to avoid oblivion. The rest evolved, as sex evolved, for reproduction is a direct product of the primal drive, a fundamental factor in survival.'

'The primal drive in the beginning is not yet soul, as the amoeba is not yet man.'

'Soul and matter are subject to the same laws of evolution. Soul is the essence of that law – survive. Every single permutation of life form has evolved because of that one, unmitigating law. The facets of the soul that we call love, creativity, mind, instinct, have all evolved as adjuncts to survival.'

'And the reasoning mind is man's heritage because of the implacability of that law.'

'Yes. The predecessor of the mind had no claws or fighting teeth. It was think or perish. I am here, and you were once here, only because that predecessor learned to think.'

The afternoon has gone. Another day has been occupied, but not without some cost. Meditation costs nothing; the mere contemplation of my navel, however, is not occupation and I'm not versed in the practice of it. But the writing is fulfilling, and there is the cost, for as it consumes time it also consumes space on the paper, as well as my precious pencils. It is difficult just to stop. I want to doodle and record almost every random thought. It is an exercise of restraint not to write.

I see my spider has returned to his new web. I wonder what is his compulsion.

*　　*　　*

I am going to go to Reef Four today. It is nearly noon and I've been gathering resolution since before the dawn. Already I've swum over the shallow reef; it was a preliminary exercise. It was intended to be a preliminary exercise. No, it is foolishness to lie to oneself, although it's partly true. I would have swum out further if the determination had been more firmly cemented, but it wasn't; at that time it was a fragmented thing and it didn't survive the first onslaught of phantoms. But since that time I have welded the fragments into a stronger determination. My will is in the ascendancy. Weakness will be conquered. I am strong. I understand my fears and, knowing them, can exercise control. It was only a very small shark.

It wasn't absolute failure. I encourage myself with that small comfort, although the truth is that I was defeated. There were no sharks, but the phantoms conquered. It was a swim clothed in alarm: every dart of every fish was startle to my twitching nerves, every cloud across the sun was a jerk of panic. I was too tense to swim, and progress was too impeded by the starts of constant trepidation. I didn't turn and flee, but there was a realisation of defeat, and it was a retreat of an accepting mind. Still, it isn't total despair. I did catch a lobster, and I have plans to cook it.

My fuel will be seaweed. For the past few days I've collected a quantity and spread it on the sand to dry. I feel sure that it will burn. Raw lobster is not palatable at all, and it's tough, but only a few minutes in boiling water and it becomes quite succulent.

Tomorrow I'll try again for Reef Four. Tomorrow I'll do it.

*　　　*　　　*

The seaweed doesn't burn. I still believe it would if I could generate enough heat. I cooked the lobster, but it meant using wood from the odd tree and I feel bad about it. If I continue to maim the tree it may not recover. That would be a tragedy; a tragedy for which I would be totally responsible and I couldn't stand the guilt of it. It would be murder. It is a living thing, drawing sustenance from this sterile earth, even more limited

114

than I; a quiet thing, undemanding, a part of my community. I mustn't kill it.

I can't go to Reef Four today, the weather has turned rough and wet. I admit to an inner relief, but a regret, too. I swam a little way out and caught a fish over the sand. I shall eat it uncooked. Raw fish is bearable. It is raining now and I have done my rain dance. I do it now whenever the rain begins. It is necessary to have ritual.

*   *   *

I can't see the other place. It is an overcast day and vision is limited. Nor can I hear the music, and my sureness slithers. The existence of the other place is part of my faith, the truth of it unimportant. For me it is reality. I know it may be no more than my own island, as I know there is no chance of ever reaching it, but the music I hear is not a fiction. There are times when I doubt, when I ask: 'Can sound travel so far undistorted?' My reason tells me that the melodies are a fabrication of the subconscious, an imagination, a deceit, but the voice of reason is not certitude. The rational mind can be wrong. Most often I believe. I believe in the music and I believe there are other people in the other place. Over there is company, the most precious adjunct to living. Not too far away, just as far as the horizon. Although whatever the distance, it is still too far. They might come here. Not by intent, for they would know this is a useless place, but by accident, perhaps, or just for a jaunt. Is that too improbable? Could I signal? Could I burn my precious trees in one supreme gamble, create a plume of smoke to be seen from well beyond the horizon? The answer has to be no. I couldn't do it, I wouldn't do it. Even if I were absolutely sure.

I am suffering dreadfully from toothache. I pray that I don't become ill again.

The sun was hot on me when I awoke. It was about midday then, and I'd been asleep for only two or three hours. It's a

115

powerful sun still and the air is thick, for the overcast has not completely gone. I blamed the sun for my bad dreams, but my toothache is malignant in my jaw and was most likely the basic cause of them. That and the brooding of the past several days.

It always amazed me how other peope could recall dreams in apparent clarity. I can sometimes remember a scene or part of a sequence from one of my dreams, but never the totality of them. I can't remember now how today's dream began. There was a vortex in which I was going round and round and feeling giddy to the point of sickness, an effect rotation has always had on me. That part of the dream has stayed. It was in water, but there was still a sensation of falling and breathing wasn't a problem. I passed many spectres peering curiously at me through the wall of the vortex. They were fixed there as if I were within a bottle, a huge glass bottle, and they were on stages outside. I have an impression that there were great numbers of them, but I can't recall all of them. I saw Hugo, I think. Monique, too, naked and bulbous through the swirl; she appeared many times. I felt that she was trying to tell me something. I felt terribly ill. Other people also. I knew them at the time but they haven't remained. My mouth felt big; I had a huge, grinning mouth with long fangs, many, many fangs. I was someone else looking at that frightful mouth. It was a dog's mouth and I was running through the thick water. There were packs of dogs, all with those terrible mouths, all chasing me. I could only run slowly in the clutch of the water's molten hands. There was a door. I pushed at it and it opened as if I were pushing against a chamber of oil. It was a circular door and as it opened a ring of teeth folded down from its perimeter. I woke up then, in palpitating, slimy terror as the sweat smothered me in the sunlight.

I am in the shade now, but the air is oppressive. The nausea of the dream is with me still. I can write no more.

*　　　*　　　*

I *must* go again to Reef Four. It is imperative that I vanquish the

116

terror strangling my spirit like some insidious creeper. I had another bad dream this morning. I can't recall it clearly, but there was a sequence of amputation of limbs – my limbs – with a large bow saw. The shark was small and I had only a slight fear of it in the water. I must remember that. The permeated dread in me now is of my own creating. The phantoms are of my mind. If I can create them, surely I can erase them.

The clouds have gone and the sea is calm. I can see the other place quite clearly today. So clearly it amazes me that I ever overlooked it.

'It is your fancy,' says the old man.

'It is your fancy,' says Monique.

'It is your fancy, it is your fancy, it is your fancy,' they chant together.

But it isn't my fancy. I can see it. I can hear the music, too. Now I shall listen. Later I shall swim.

Again I failed to reach Reef Four. This time it wasn't the phantoms that forced me back, however, although they were there and I was terrified. It was the current that beat me. It was strong today, not as strong as on the day of the ordeal, but too strong to risk the chance of a second one. I dived and skewered a fish on the sandy bottom, a technique that I've really perfected. The fish is of a type that is strange to me, I haven't caught its like before; larger and flatter than the usual bottom dweller. It's nearly dark now and the fish is lying there on the sand looking at me, his eyes large and bulging, luminous in the slanted light. They remind me of frog's eyes. They are fixed on me. There is malevolence in them.

'I'm sorry I killed you, fish,' I say, but he doesn't respond. There is a movement of the gills as if he isn't quite dead. 'You are dead, aren't you?' I ask. 'I hope you're not suffering there, lying so still. But your mouth doesn't move, so you can't be breathing.' He looks at me steadily.

He has very small scales, brown and unvarying, so that I have to peer hard to distinguish one from the next, but they glisten, reflecting the last, tired rays of the failing sun. His belly

117

is quite white underneath, like most bottom fish, although I can only see a strip of it now, and the hole in it where the spear emerged will have tinted the whiteness, rimming the scales in pink and making the sand dark beneath it like the hole in his back, fully black now, looking like a patch stuck on. He has a triangular head jutting rather higher than the rest of him, so that his frog's eyes would project when he burrowed into the sea floor. I can still see them as the day finally and inaudibly departs. There is little change of light, for already the moon is high. I could see it in the east long before the sun went down.

The fish continues to look at me. I can't see the malevolence in the gentler light of the moon. We stare at each other. There is a reluctance in me to move it. A strange sensation comes with the early night. There's a bond between me and this fish that I have killed. There is something beautiful in its pose on the shadowed sand, some property of shade and shape that I like, that is part of the bond. It is dead but its spirit, its soul, has not, with its physical death, ceased to be, not yet. It has a force, a most gentle and aesthetic force, and that, too, is part of the bond. Its spirit has settled on me, it clings to my own spirit to maintain for a little while longer the perception of being.

'Fish, I shouldn't have killed you.' His eyes are huge. The moon is curtained and the fish has merged with its shadows. Only his eyes are distinct, great balls of wet malignity. The mood has changed. Suddenly the rapport has evaporated. I sweat. My will is in that sweat, leaking from me. Why don't I stand up and shed this shrouding cloy? But the bond remains, linking it to me. The sensation is still with me although its nature has changed, and my will is only clam.

*　　*　　*

I lost touch with all reality then. I stopped writing and, re-membering it, I wonder how I wrote so much. Of course there was more time involved than the writing itself absorbed. There were long periods of just looking at the fish in a sort of mutual mesmerism, and then I felt a sadness and then later came the communion, soon after the end of day. It was quite some time after that, that the evil came.

The eyes of the fish grew bigger and bigger, hooded eyes with only darkness below like the heads of monks, cowled in the gloom. I could feel the malevolence as a pressure. The moon had vanished. The eyes were overwhelming. I put my arms over my head and rolled over. I have an idea that I was shrieking: 'Go away, go away!' I lay for some time with my head on the sand, buried beneath my arms. My arms were my shield. I knew that, if I lifted them, the thick darkness would be waiting. The sound of the sea began to intrude into my senses above my limp and wilted being. I forced myself to listen, to concentrate on that sound, to exclude the waiting malevolence from my consciousness. I looked out beneath my arms. The fish lay there, its mouth an arm's length from my own. It smiled. I saw the teeth; twin rows of teeth, dripping with mucus, the slime connecting the rows with ribbons between the jaws. Jaws opening wider and wider. Rows and rows of teeth. The fish thrashing on the sand. A monstrous black length of it, fins like scimitars.

In the morning it was simply a dead fish. I took it and threw it far out into the sea. That act and this recording of the experience have allowed a certain smother of reason to soothe my nerves. But it was not just a bad dream. I lived it, awake, aware and conscious.

'It was an hallucination,' says Muller. I am glad of his company, even if his words are disturbing. I understand how my loneliness was affecting my mind with the projection of wraiths like Muller and Deirdre, giving them substance and voice, but that isn't madness; the comprehension of it keeps it within the bounds of sanity. The fish was something different, although clearly it is related to the shark.

'Am I so close to madness, old man?'

'Madness is a comparative term. From where do you draw your comparisons?'

Always the teacher, ever the dialectic.

'Don't be evasive, Muller. I've read of the symptoms of

madness; I don't need comparisons.'

'But your reading has been in a social framework, its observations relative to society.' He has on his nightshirt. I find that apparel very reassuring, somehow, and I need reassurance today.

'Yes, of course it doesn't matter if I go mad here, alone, with nobody to assess my sanity. But when rescue comes I don't want to be found a gibbering maniac.'

'Rescue! You still believe in rescue, then?'

'Yes. Yes, I do. I have to. See that other island over there, there are people on that island. One day a party will visit here.'

'What island?'

'That island there, from where the music comes.' I see it so clearly this morning, a definite piece of land interrupting the blanket expanse of sea.

Muller looks. He says: 'If you see an island there, then there is one. If you hear music, then there is music.'

'And if I saw a monster fish in the night lying on the sand, then there was a monster fish.'

He looks at me, solid and sharp, not an illusion. He says: 'But it was just a small fish you threw into the sea this morning.'

*   *   *

I am waiting to go to Reef Four, but the current persists. I am convinced of the current. Yet reaching Reef Four has become so much of an aim for me now that the phantoms are surely insignificant. I dive and swim with much of my old confidence on the nearer reefs, and yesterday I slept easily. There were no nightmares, no hallucinations. It is as if the night of the monstrous fish was the climax of an obsession. I was spineless and weak, but through it all there was one straw to clutch at, in that my mind was always seeking to understand; and so at the last I feel a sense of victory. Last night, then, with the obsession erased, the music came again. It sounded so close, so sharp, I was constrained to call out. If I can hear them, surely they could hear me. That's foolishness, of course; the music comes to me on the wind, a wind that would immediately disperse my voice in the wrong direction. But I enjoyed the night. Deirdre came and danced for me for a while in the spasms of moonlight, but she left as quickly and magically as she came. She was pleasant, but I prefer the music.

Why is it that I can't talk to her as I do to Muller? Is it because I don't see women as cerebral creatures? Of course they are, some of them, although my lovers have never been particularly so. Is that why I rarely consider them in that light? That is a terrible admission of bigotry, but reflecting now on my past relationships with women, carnal or otherwise, I see that my bigotry is nearly truth. Is this bigotry an error common to all men, or is it an especial trait of mine? Do all men see women in a purely physical light? It seems to me that, when I've been newly introduced to a woman, although the possibility of an affair with her might be remote, still I would tend to view her in a physical context. Do women realise that? I suppose they must. Deirdre represents nothing to me other than carnal desire. Women are so much more than that, and one's reasoning knows it, but there is something more ingrained in man than reason, a dominant syndrome that has little relevance in an educated society. It accounts in part for the reason why my recollections of women in my life are more photographic than substantial, images that reveal little of the complexities of personality beneath the flat record of physical features. That is why I can't reach Deirdre, for she reflects truly my attitude towards women. I fail to reach her as I failed to reach the essence of any of my women. My relationships were fundamentally calls of the flesh; not without emotion entirely, indeed emotion was at times intense. I see, though, that people, not only women, are more than mere physical drives, however much the emotions are entangled with those drives. People are victims of evolution, victims of environment, victims of education, victims of their heredity, victims of the primal heritage, and also victims of the age they were born in. These are the inescapable shackles of living, the indelible elements of all human personality.

'Physical features are equally important,' says my mentor in his bland, soft voice. He stands over by the lapping tide getting the hem of his nightshirt wet. 'Consider the idea of beauty. Those gifted with it are given confidence along with their features.'

'Well, I would consider beauty part of their genetic heritage. Besides, beauty is a thing of fashion and a thing of opinion. What may be considered beautiful in one age and one society is not necessarily so classed in another.'

'True, but it has to be judged by the age and society in which it exists. It can break the shackles of living by its own excellence.'

'Yes, but no more than any other gift, less so, perhaps, than genius. Beauty is only a detail; I accept that it gives confidence and so affects personality in that small way, but confidence is not much on its own; neither beauty nor confidence can affect genetic patterns. They will not give one control of courage, temper or reflexes, and personality is so much more a matter of courage and temper and reflexes. It is fashioned of the traumas of childhood, the grapplings of adolescence, of opportunity, of circumstance, of temperament, and above all of ancestry.'

'It is composed of selfishness, nothing more nor less,' he snaps, moving away from the water and sitting down just below me. Muller has changed lately. He is certainly less pedantic, but also more emphatic.

'That's the effect of the primary instinct for survival, the element that turned chemistry into life.'

'Yes. Man can be no other way.'

I don't know that I fully accept that. I study the old man, still there, shrivelled in his nightshirt.

I say: 'Is it not possible for man to be taught the control of his inborn selfishness?'

'It is never considered. Leaders, teachers, governments never make decisions based upon the characteristics of the people they control, even if some of them do recognise the elements of character. Decisions are determined by ideology or by expediency, with no consideration of human reaction.'

'What about you? You were a teacher.'

He looks at me with those moist eyes in that crumpled face and I realise that this wraith is not Muller at all. He never has been Muller. He is just the reflection of prejudice in myself, prejudice and confusion. He is the compost of my subconscious mind. 'I never gave it a thought,' he says.

'So my selfish attitude towards women is as much from my education, or the failings of that education, as it is from an ancient imprint on my psyche.'

'Don't blame education. Your attitude was established generations before you were born; it is in the genes of your soul.' It is a terribly powerful statement from such a withered form.

'I'm the same as all men, then?'

'Why not?'

'Because education does develop attitude – education and example. These must overlie and suppress the genetic traits. The genetic endowment is but one factor in the formation of a character, though it is, admittedly, strong in its influence.'

'In the final analysis it's the dominating one.'

'Then it's fortunate that man rarely has to face a final analysis.'

'Some say he has to face it after death.'

I can't stand the old man when he drifts into such rutted statements. He knows this and there's no need to dismiss him. When I look up again he isn't there. It's not right to blame him, though. He is simply reflecting the clichés of my upbringing. I was brought up in the basic concept of the existence of God. Inherent in that concept was that there would come a time after death, when the 'Big Book' would be opened and the sins of my life would be weighed against the good deeds; my Maker would sit in judgement upon me. And although I have long since discarded this absurd portrayal of the final analysis, the power of such teaching on a young mind has left its debris. Debris which constantly distorts the purity of any other stream of thought. Man's philosophy must be an amalgam of clichés, as hybrid as man himself. I fear that I can't escape that social heritage, any more than I can escape the primal one.

*   *   *

Ten days have passed since I last scratched words with my dwindling pencil. Days of some rain, some wind, a lot of discomfort, two games of chess, and a trip to Reef Four. That was two days ago. There was no shark and only a lingering disquiet in the place of phantoms. I went out there again today. It's difficult to express what the place means to me. It's my major source of relief from the endless monotony. It's a sublime place with a beauty that's more than just solace for my soul, although that's its greatest benefit. It has a beauty of constant discovery; because its loveliness is organic it can never be the same; and sometimes it is bright when the sunlight is strong and the water is clear, and sometimes it is ghostly, shadowed and unreal like walking through a forest in the twilight; and often it is a moving, swirling, shifting garden of colour, when the seaweed changes from brown to green in the rolling sweeps of the current and fish glitter in sudden movements, and shoals of fish turn and veer and turn again in magical unison like a conducted orchestra. Then it is really a place of magic, of enchantment.

After such days there are inevitably nights of music. This day was such a day, and tonight there will be rhapsodies. I've seen lights on the island. There, so close, so very close, are the delights of society. The music will be tangible; there will be pretty girls in pretty dresses; there will be perfume and wine, books and pictures and flowers. Oh, I'd love to hold a flower, and I'd love to smell the smell of grass. I want to lie in grass, to bury my face in the green, green, green of it, to walk without shoes or socks in the dew. I think I'd like that as much as the arms of a woman. Ideally I'd like to lie in the grass – long grass, as it is before hay is cut – within the arms of a woman, within the legs of a woman, within the smell and the warmth and the hair and the breasts of a woman, with the grass all around, and hear the sounds of a meadow: the bees and the crickets and the scurryings of little things. I miss the meadows. Here I have not one blade of grass to build a dream on, just the sand and a scrawny tree and, up there, coconut leaves. They are green, definitely green, but not the green of a meadow, not the glistening deep green of grass in the spring, the acres of green that cause men to stop and look and drink it in. There is in man a profound communion with grazing land, a kind of dreaminess, an urge to stroll and kneel and feel the grass, a contentment, a syndrome that directs urban droves into the country in the pauses from asphalt lives. It is a need, uncomprehended and beyond analysis. It is a need that the anaemic, faded green of my coconut leaves cannot satisfy.

But the fruit is swelling most satisfactorily.

✳   ✳   ✳

There was another storm, a most dreadful assault by sea and wind; a terrifying, crashing sea, immense waves thundering like giant angry fists, battering the island back into the depths; and the wind howling, flattening me, flattening the trees, tearing the roof from my shelter, while I lay huddled between the walls nursing the spider in my cupped hand. The wind shrieked its spite for perhaps three quarters of the day and half the night. The sea is pounding even now, less wild but violent still. I am wet through with rain and sea, and just now low in spirit. I'm shivering. I have toothache again, and my only food is raw shellfish. The storm has washed away my plottings of the sky, my chess game, and all but stripped the odd tree of its meagre leaves. The palm fronds are shredded. But I see that the coconuts themselves have survived. Even that doesn't cheer me. What is the use? Why bother? The storm has beaten me down, stripped me like the odd tree, only the primal imperative remains. In that Muller is right. There is in me yet a germ of resistance that all my reason, all my dispirit will not eradicate. It means that I shall survive, although at this moment I don't care. Not much.

Even not caring poses a problem. It would not be easy to precipitate death in this situation. Drowning can't be contemplated. Cutting one's wrists requires a particular type of courage that I certainly lack. Starving would be too slow, the process outlasting one's determination. Poisoning would be possible if I knew of a source lethal enough; no doubt there are poisonous species of fish, but which ones and how to catch them are insoluble questions. There is some irony in my deliberations on the problem; I, who have struggled so hard for so long to live, can't now visualise an easy way to die. But I don't want to die; it is but an idle speculation – the primal heritage glimmers yet. Still, the irony has a certain wry humour and that helps lift me from my depression.

I shall attempt to light a fire. That is a decision of some resolution, and some sacrifice. It will mean burning a few pages of this book, something I have resisted doing since I first stepped onto this futile beach. And I shall have to burn some of the remaining branches from my dear, desecrated tree. Its wood is green but it does burn well and, with enough heat, surely the seaweed will ignite. It's wet now, though, and it will require a very hot fire to dry it out. This is my resolve. I realise the odd tree may not recover, but I shall have my fire. Just as soon as the sun appears.

*   *   *

I have my fire. The odd tree is just a skeleton. The storm took its leaves and I took its limbs. It is not dead. It has struggled in its own determination not to die through many onslaughts of the wind, through the endless days of drying sun, waterless and with the most frugal source of nourishment, and it has survived. Even now, perhaps, it will respond to the urges of its own basic tenacity and live. I am the mutilant. I am penitent.

But I have the biggest fire yet achieved here. The seaweed, once alight, gives off a lot of heat. I have cooked a fish, a crab and a lobster. This is luxury indeed, especially as the weather remains cold, the wind is blowing and there is dampness in the air – not quite rain, more of a suspended wetness moved by the wind. There was an hour or two of sun this morning, though, which enabled me to start my fire. I used four pages from this book to achieve the initial blaze. Now I'm closeted in heat. Vagaries of the wind blow smoke into my eyes quite frequently, but mainly I simply sit in comfort and stare dreamily at the embers. This must be almost the oldest occupation of man in his leisure hours, staring into a fire and permitting the slumberous visions to flicker like the flames. I have done it many times before, in more organised and more accompanied times, often with Hugo. We would grill sausages and cook potatoes in the ash. We would smoke and make arcs of light with glowing sticks in the woodland dark. But mostly we would talk together, quietly – vague and unrecorded conversations that brushed but lightly upon our sensitivities – or sit in pleasant silence, each thinking thoughts alone, sometimes poking the fire or idly turning a burning log. And the mantles of our individual hush would merge in unspoken recognition of company, in a contentment of presence and fire in the dark.

Surely this contentment, this feeling of security, is something so old in the substance of man that it must be a basic part of his soul. It must be related to the early conquest of his environment. With no natural weapons, with just stones and sticks to discourage predators, the control of fire gave him possibly the greatest leap forward towards supremacy of any single technical discovery of any man at any time. It gave him not only a superior means of protection, but so much more in the capacity to defeat even the fiercest of beasts, even the savage bear of the caves. Thus the basic warp was implanted in his soul and, stronger still, a reciprocal warp was implanted in the essence of beasts, a wariness of the creature called 'man'. So man sits now, gazing idly into his fire, his creation, his possession, and the security of countless progenitors sitting before their fires settles comfortingly and comfortably about his shoulders.

'You think a great deal about your ancestors,' remarks the wraith – I hesitate to call him Muller any more. He takes

127

Hugo's place to my left, hunching his skinny arms about his equally skinny knees, his nightshirt pulled up above them.

'I suppose it's my solitude. It focuses attention on every sensation that I feel; then the question arises why I feel that particular way, and the causes must lie in heredity.'

'You seem to ignore, or choose not to consider, the effects of your own life on those feelings. It can't all be ancestral.'

'Those effects are merely social effects. My reactions now are more deeply rooted.'

He is rubbing his shins up and down with all the fingers of each hand, slowly, rocking slightly as he does so. My mother would do that, sitting before the kitchen stove. I remember she had a series of blue circles on her legs, caused by the heat on her skin. Her brown stockings would be rolled down around her ankles and her dress pulled up like Muller's nightshirt. There was the same rocking motion and the fingers sliding up and down in unison. 'Are all instincts a form of genetic memory?' he asks.

'Why not? It is a mistake to think that inheritance is merely a matter of physical and mental factors.'

'Yes, it's certainly more than that. We inherit the ancestral and evolved characteristics of the soul, from the beginning of all life to the present time, and our individual inheritances are as variable as our faces. But the soul is not the receptacle of memory.'

There is not much flame on the fire now, but plenty of emberglow. The colours are gold and black and red and orange, and they move and interchange. The heat is quite intense. Muller, I will call him that, keeps rubbing his legs. His fingers have big knuckles and there is chalk under his nails. 'The soul *is* in fact the receptacle of memory if one accepts that the mind is part of the soul,' I murmur.

'Then it would follow that all living things have a mind.'

'Oh, most certainly. But it's a matter of degree, isn't it? It's also a matter of content. We mustn't assume that the human mind is the only pattern for the faculty. Why should it be?'

'Does a tree think?'

128

'In terms of the human mind? No, but because it has life, it has that other factor besides chemistry, it has soul, and a mind that, in our fixed concept of what mind is, we cannot comprehend.'

'And memory?'

'Not as we understand it, but in some way, some part of its "livingness" must be memory. There is something that is recorded upon its genetic content that, over countless eons of its evolution, stamps the pattern of its behaviour, of its responses to conditions.'

The sky is particularly black tonight. I can't see the moon, and only one star right over the northern horizon. The wind is abating but eddies still occur, stirring the fire and making quick, jumping flames. The smoke is causing my eyes to water. The old man seems impervious to it. He says: 'If the soul carries memory from generation to generation, why don't we remember everything from the inception of man until now?'

'I suppose the capacity to carry all the meaningless incidents of untold meaningless lives does not exist. The primal heritage is concerned with only one imperative. Only those memories that aid its basic motive become a part of it, exactly as physical evolution works. Selectivity, if you like.'

'The discovery of fire, for example.'

'Oh yes, but it isn't so simple, of course. Obviously the discovery of fire and the benefits of fire were passed on by an educational process through countless generations. The mechanics of it would not affect the soul. But the emotions generated by it, such as security, confidence, contentment, perhaps even the feeling of superiority, these were the factors affecting the evolution of the soul. It is this memory, the emotional one, not that of consciousness, that surfaces when man sits around his fire.'

The fire is getting low, imploding and collapsing bit by bit. It's little more now than red cinders on the sand. Our conversation and the writing of it have been spasmodic, and probably in reality not always spoken. It has lasted over two hours, I would think. And that is the wonder of dreaming before a fire.

129

Surely it was the nightly hours of so long ago that exercised the ancestral mind. Man is man because of fire. It gave him status in the world of the predator, it gave him the potential for superiority, and it gave him, finally and inevitably, a thinking mind.

I can't have another fire. There are no more sacrifices to make.

*　　*　　*

Reef Four has again extracted payment from me. I transgressed and have already paid the penalty. Reef Four has to be an inviolate place, that was my rule, my self-imposition. I deviated from that imposition, and I have suffered because of it. That suffering must be considered as retribution. The return swim to shore was anguish, not the mindless endurance of my previous ordeal, but sheer physical agony and that endurance needed to withstand it. No delights are available on this Earth without a price; consider love, consider children, consider the joys of sport. Reef Four also has its price.

I really had no need of the lobster, but it was especially big and I was tempted. So I dived. It evaded me as they usually do in the open, and with one or two flips of its abdomen vanished into a crevice. I noted the spot, surfaced for breath and dived again. It was still in the crevice, wedging itself back and waggling its feelers. The reef is such a tranquil place, that one is pervaded with a sense of complete peace, a serenity; apart from the one shark there has never been any hint of danger; one's natural caution is sublimated. There is no hostility there, and even now I believe that. I was an aggressor. I intruded and the reef reacted. It was plain carelessness, really. I thrust my left hand into the crevice without even taking the precaution of examining the surrounding niches.

The movement was so incredibly swift that although I saw my hand at all times, I didn't see the eel attack. It was just there, suddenly, its teeth buried in my hand, thrashing about, wrenching and tearing on my sinews, a thick, green writhing

thing, covered in dark spots, and the blood was flowing, also green at that depth. It was a pain like the pain of fire. I jerked repeatedly before tearing my hand free and kicking myself to the surface. It wasn't possible to study the wound in the water. The blood flowed freely, red now at the surface, and I clutched the wrist with my other hand to try to stop it. Looking down to the crevice I couldn't see the eel. I began to swim for shore using only my legs, still clutching the wrist, but the blood continued to flow and the pain was growing more and more intense as the initial shock wore off. There was a current running across the sandy area, not really strong but I would need to use my arms. I felt a great reluctance to let go of my wrist, as if that grip was saving my life force from draining away. I did let it go, though, forcing common sense to take control. At first I swam holding my wounded hand tucked into the armpit of the right arm, but that made swimming most difficult and achieved very little in helping the hand. It was necessary to use both arms and allow the blood to flow.

How can I describe that swim? Only in terms of agony. I had to endure it, there was no other way. The suffering arm was feeble and at the end did little to assist. It was molten pain. Yet I did endure it, somehow, and the distance was finally covered. By that time the bleeding had stopped. Sitting on the beach, again holding my wrist and moaning as if the escape of sound could ease the pain, I examined the damage. My left hand is torn severely, very swollen now, but on the beach I could see the sinews stripped. It throbs continually and I can't move the arm, but with care it shouldn't bleed again, although the flesh is so ragged I am amazed the blood has stopped at all. It requires to be stitched, of course, but that action is beyond me. In time it will heal, I suppose, as it is, with the flesh twisted and the shape of my hand distorted for ever. I have put it in a sling made from my singlet so that I don't bang it in my sleep. I doubt if I'll sleep much for a day or two.

*   *   *

These writings have been a great source of occupation for me, as well as a means of flattening the swells of fancy, a solace and a salve to unsteady emotions. They were intended always to be no more than a personal record of my actions and my thoughts in this total solitude. But lately I feel that I'm writing to somebody, for some intimate person who will understand, without the slightest sense of who that might be. It is as if I am trying to tell that unknown identity something that it's necessary to tell, and that, of course, is a vanity. Yet the feeling exists and it has become almost a central part of my attitude to this chronicle. It also represents, perhaps, my first conscious acknowledgement that I'm going to die here. This record has assumed an immense value to me, almost a vital one. I want it to survive even though I may not, as it is, with its shame and its intimate admissions, but also with its small triumphs and its dubious meditations. I can see the other island there, quite clearly. I can see that it has palm trees, more than here, and other vegetation. I think I can discern buildings. At night there are lights, and always the music. But if I do die before they come here I want them to find this record.

Thoughts of death do occupy me, but not as morbidly as my obsession with the shark. My hand is paining me very badly. It is infected and the poison has swollen not only the hand but also the wrist. The pus oozes and congeals around the wounds. Sometimes I vomit. Food is not easy to get now, for I can't swim, so the sickness is probably as much repugnance to raw shellfish as the actual effect of the infection. I have to wade in the shallows to collect the shellfish. I do that in sweat and giddiness and nausea, the wrist throbbing and my legs without strength, but it is necessary, for there is no other source of food. My left arm, of course, is useless, and the armpit holds the massive lump of a distended gland. I feel that one or two coconuts would be ready to open; it would be premature but their liquid would surely be beneficial. My body needs nutrition or the infection will take too strong a hold. However, I can't climb the trees so I can but look up and think about it. It appears, then, that unless the infection kills me by its own assault, it could do so by depriving me of the ability to feed myself adequately. These are my thoughts of death. I am calm about it and resigned as I write of it. I just hope that there isn't too much pain.

*   *   *

There is a lot of pain. Oh my God, how can I endure it? The whole of my left arm and shoulder throbs remorselessly. I don't sleep; sleep just isn't possible. I can't eat. I drink a great deal, so much, that I must soon empty my reservoirs. I can't write at all well, my pencils are blunt and it is impossible to sharpen them with one hand; even holding the paper in position is a feat of will, but I must record what I can.

It is not like the previous infection; it is behaving quite differently. My brain has remained clear, although I wish it were otherwise. Unconsciousness would be a blessing. There is no high fever, either, in spite of a definite malaise and a weakness in my limbs. I am able to stand, but it is an action of mental determination so demanding that I prefer to crawl on one hand and my knees to the drinking spots. That is my one activity, otherwise I remain unmoving. When will the torment be over?

I can write no more.

*   *   *

Five days. The anguish is over. I still hurt and I'm very weak, but the infection has certainly gone, by what miracle of recovery is beyond my understanding. My hand pains and I can't move the fingers, but I can sleep. I fell asleep yesterday – it was after midday – and didn't wake till mid-morning. I'll eat something soon, not much, for I lack confidence in my stomach, but a little, and later, if I feel up to it, I'll get a coconut. So again death has neglected me. He probably doesn't know I'm here. After all, this is a forgotten place.

133

The green coconuts are quite sweet. They are full of liquid and have no meat. There is no need to husk them: the shell is soft at the eyes and the drink is much cooler than the water in the pools. I picked only one, but I also ate the entrails of a sea-urchin. It hadn't occurred to me previously that sea-urchins could be a source of food, but in fact they are quite succulent. Sea-urchins are singularly spiny creatures and I've always taken pains to avoid them. Some areas of the shallow reefs abound with them, but it was sheer chance that prompted me to eat one. I had a tentative swim this morning – actually more of a stooped walk at the fringes of the sea wearing the mask. I attempted to lift a rock with an abalone attached, but my left arm is still feeble and I let the rock go. It fell onto an urchin, crushing it. Inside it there was a thick yellow fluid exactly like custard. Within seconds the fluid was being assailed by little fish, some coming quickly from the limits of my vision to share in the feast. Very soon the sea-urchin was nothing but a broken shell; no vestige of the yellow fluid remained and the fish dispersed.

So I collected a sea-urchin for myself in lieu of the abalone, gingerly, but I discovered that if handled without pressure one can pick them up with little risk of puncture. On shore I broke off the spines, opened the case and scooped out the fluid with a mussel shell. There was a small hesitation before eating it, but I found it very tasty and my stomach did not reject it. Now there is just a little bit more variety to my limited menu, and to my existence. I must investigate other sources of sea food. Perhaps starfish are edible. What of seaweed itself? I do recall reading that there are people who eat seaweed. There are also squid and octopi in the water, and I know they can be eaten, if I could only devise a method of catching them; they do move very swiftly.

I think it's going to rain. The sun shone unhindered in immaculate skies during my illness, but now there are gathering clouds. I'll be able to do my rain dance; I'm fit enough for that. The rain dance owes nothing to ancestry or genetic impulse; it is a conscious act of deliberate ritual, but still one I find profoundly satisfying. I understand many peoples throughout the world perform rain dances – American Indians, some African tribes, the aborigines of Australia, natives of Burma, Malaya and other Asian lands – so there must be some universal impulse associated with rainfall; I have even heard that some species of ape also do a rain dance, but whatever the source of their behaviour, my dance has no connection with it. Mine is a calculated ceremony, a distinctly cerebral performance; I have borrowed only the idea. The idea, in fact, must be a very ancient one, but the tradition has been passed down the generations by education only; it has no survival value so has not imprinted itself upon man's soul. Modern man certainly feels no impulse to perform ritual gyrations either to bring on rain or to celebrate its arrival. I have felt no such impulse, either. The creation of my dance was dependant entirely upon the relief of boredom. The onset of rain only serves to give it meaning. It is a cavorting, raucous, sensual performance, done in nakedness with the cold of the starting rain sharp on the skin. The skin twitches and a sense of release fills me. I sing and cry at the limits of my voice. I leap and run as if jumping fences; I kneel on the sand and fling my arms and my face to the spilling sky; I prance and whirl and arc my hips forward, male and tumid, increasingly forceful as a frenzy grows. Something primitive does grip me then, induced by the dance; it never prompts it but it does take over and I willingly let it. I lose conscious record of what I'm doing then. There are cymbals and drums and chanting in the shadows. There is the smell of sweat and genitals, and giddiness. There is hair swinging about me. And voices, wailing, hailing and crying in my ears: 'Yes, yes, yes . . .'

Until the giddiness makes me ill and I fall crumpled and spent. And I am a quiet whimpering man, crying from my loneliness. The ritual is over and the rain washes over me.

But it isn't raining yet and I shall not dance until the first drops fall.

Why doesn't man have more protection from the rain? Why doesn't he have fur like other mammals? Apes have fur. Man has a ridiculous overabundance of hair on his head as if nature tried to compensate for his nakedness by growing a coat from his crown. If there was a common forebear to both apes and man, did he have locks like a man or fur like an ape? 'Muller, are you there? Can you answer this question?'

'I never taught you of such things.' Muller settles himself comfortably on the sand, tucking his nightgown carefully under his scrawny shanks. Evidently no pontifications today.

'There must have been an evolutionary significance in the factor of nakedness,' I muse. 'Without fur, man would certainly have been prompted to hunt, wouldn't he?'

'There might be something in that. Other primates don't hunt.'

The old fellow is really being exceedingly agreeable.

I go on: 'The more furless man's progenitors became, the more they were compelled to hunt; not for food, because primates can exist very well without meat, but for clothing. That's why the other apes remain basically vegetarian. Their forebears were never prompted to hunt.'

'So meat eating evolved simply as a by-product of an initial need for body covering.' He speaks neatly today, no slobbering, the words clear and precise, just as I remember him. 'That's all very well, but I have one objection.' I sit so smugly in my theory that I feel an automatic resentment of any suggestion that there's a weakness in it.

'What's that?' I snap.

'At that stage of human evolution, this hypothetical forebear didn't have the tools to remove the skins of beasts, even if he had the weapons to kill them in the first place.' Silly old sod. But he has a point. I am moved to defend the concept.

'Couldn't a troop of them have disembowelled their prey? They could have attacked an antelope, say, with sticks and stones. And having killed it, weren't their teeth large enough to rend the hide?'

'It's your theory.' The old fool is not accepting it. He always

136

did have pedantic attitudes.

'If they were advanced enough to hunt, then they were advanced enough to remove the hides,' I insist. But he is silent. 'That may even have been the origin of tool making,' I continue, warming to the whole theme now as a range of possibilities begins to open up.

But there is no more time to explore them, for at this moment the first drops of rain have landed on my scribbled words and I must do my rain dance.

Editor's Note
At this juncture in the journal there are pages missing – the last few pages of the book, in fact. It can only be assumed they are the pages he used to start his fire, but as more than the four he stated are missing it is probable that he used others to make a later fire. It is not mentioned. From this point in the narrative the chronology is subject to some interpretation, for most of the writing is around the borders of the pages already used, and there is little guide to the continuity other than the sense of it. The writing is cramped and often blurred, as if the pencils were used to the limits of bluntness. One can only imagine the tediousness of this method of writing. Unfortunately, much of it is repetitious, more a record of what was eaten and the climatic conditions than an account of behaviour. There were further, apparently uneventful, trips to Reef Four, although one of note is on record; more conversations with his spectral teacher, which are not always decipherable owing to some damage sustained to the page edges; and it seems another wild storm occurred, but once again much of this section is indecipherable. So, of necessity, some editing has had to be done in this latter part of the chronicle. However, it is emphasised that scrupulous care has been taken not to alter the essential nature of the writing. Indeed, no words of the writer have been altered at all, although some assumptions have been made, and much repetition has been omitted.

Actually, unless some writing was torn out with the missing pages, he wrote very little for a period that seems to have lasted for a few weeks, because his next series of entries records a regular use of coconuts.

My shelter is now as complete as my ambitions require. It's about five feet high and six feet long, open at both ends, although I can close either end off with a shutter of woven palm leaves, depending on the direction of the weather. The roof is close to rainproof now, a composite of the four turtle shells and palm leaves. There are still some chinks between the stacked rocks of the wall, but sand is piled against each side and that is a very effective means of protecting the walls, although it is necessary to repair these banks quite frequently. I am confident the shelter will withstand any further storms; the roof is weighted down and my shutter will prevent any lifting of the roof from the inside.

It is a still day today, no wind at all. The sea is like a pale green fabric, stretched but not entirely smooth. The sky is totally blue and the horizon a distinct straight line. It is also hot. The island fries. Four days now without wind or cloud. I sit and stare at the sea. The habit of mindless hours will easily capture me if I allow it, as it has done during the past few days. There are disturbances on the surface of the sea well out from the island and I suppose there are porpoises there. Too far away to be sure. I haven't seen porpoises close to the island at all, although once some passed near enough for recognition.

I see the other island clearly on such a day. It looks larger than this one, with a hill rising in the middle of it. A lot of vegetation with dark spots in the sky moving above it – they are obviously birds. Other sounds apart from music come to me across the intervening distance: bird cries, people singing, people laughing, dogs barking; social sounds, living sounds, the sounds of interwoven lives. The island seems to be coming closer, but that must be just an improvement in eyesight due to

138

the constant exercise of gazing to the limits of my vision. I am, or that is to say, I was, once quite short-sighted, which explains why I never saw the other island for many months. My vision has plainly improved.

'It's a mirage,' says Muller.

It is true that sometimes the island does seem to float above the sea, but that is just a trick of distance and heat haze. I won't debate the issue with the old man; he represents merely a subconscious doubt, a refusal to accept the element of hope. Indeed, it is a familiar sally of hopelessness, but too tentative now to challenge my confidence. The other place is there. I am decidedly sure of that.

*   *   *

The last day and night have been a benumbed, unfeeling time. I haven't moved. I just sit staring senselessly at my feet. Empty. I am absolutely empty. This is the emptiness beyond despair, the uncaring emptiness of total defeat.

I suppose that the writing of these words indicates that there is still some will within me, somewhere, smothered and trying to be under the weight of emptiness, some germ of primary motive. It isn't hope, it can never again be hope, but even in apathy there is some response to an undefined subliminal drive to record.

Again it was Reef Four that extracted its price. The place is so serene, so undemanding, and all I do is go there and look. But still there is a price. Neptune is an usurer. The days have been quite without motion; they are often that way recently, without wind, and hot, and the water is as clear as I have ever known it. I could see further and deeper than on any previous day. I was entranced. Of course I was entranced. I explored beyond the reef and dived to the limits of my lungs down the sloping wall of the reef. There were other types of fish further down, larger fish, but peaceful and unconcerned at my spasmodic presence; unaggressive fish, observing me with the same curiosity with which I studied them. I was under the surface as much as above, and on the surface my ears were full of sea. Or I should have heard the sound earlier.

But suddenly I was aware of it, a droning even through the wetness of my ears. There were moments, minutes even, when recognition eluded me. I knew only that it was a familiar sound, not music which is the only sound I hear other than the wind.

A sound in the air. It was coming from the air. I looked up in such a state of immediate excitement that I momentarily forgot to swim and my face promptly went under so that I swallowed water. I was choking and attempting to shout; I was waving my arms while trying to swim, and I felt as if I might explode with the emotion billowing within me. It was an aeroplane. Close enough to see clearly its shape and colour. I trod water and waved and waved and waved. I shouted continually, incomprehensible cries, knowing the uselessness of it in a strange side chapel of my brain, but too jubilant to stop until I could only croak. The 'plane was passing my island. Surely they could see me. Oh God, let them see me! I should be on shore burning everything there was to burn.

Was it too late? I swam hard. Never in all my life have I swum as hard. I reached the shore within minutes. But the plane had gone. The sky was a virgin blue and there was no sound at all.

I must have stood and stared at that hateful purity for perhaps an hour. That can only be a guess. It was a suspension of time. It was then that the emptiness started. I left my hope in the sea, there on Reef Four. But the reef will be utterly indifferent.

* * *

'Why don't you pray?' asks Muller, as compassionately as his slobber will permit. I know the old reprobate was a complete agnostic himself. He must have concealed it well from the school authorities for they would not have approved, but the student body knew and admired him greatly for it, somewhat guiltily, though, for at that age any deviant thought was heresy, and our green minds were already being constricted by traditional dogma.

'Who do I pray to?'

'To any deity you choose.' It's a windy day and somewhat cool. I find it very pleasant after the heat of the last two weeks. Muller wears a pullover, a grey, grubby garment with a V-neck exposing the top buttons of his nightshirt. The sleeves disappear into equally grubby grey gloves through which several fingernails emerge at the worn extremities. He scratches his armpit through the gloves.

'Would a god listen? How can the prayers of untold thousands of individuals all receive attention at one time?'

'Isn't that part of the mystery of the godhead?' He is serious enough, although there is a note of withheld ridicule in his voice.

'Do you mean the Christian God?'

'I mean any god. There's surely only one, isn't there? The God of Islam, the God of Buddha, the Christian one, aren't they all the same?'

'Not in the manner of worship. The ethics are also different, as well as the mechanics.'

He sniffs. 'That's merely the reflections of differing cultures.' His shoulders move stiffly, with great effort. It is a shrug. 'Because men differ in their approach to God, that doesn't mean that God himself is a variable.'

'No, I suppose not. But God is a concept, and concepts do differ.' His grey pullover stirs a chord of memory. I try to develop that in a separate chamber of my mind while considering my thoughts on God. I have for a long time classed myself as an unbeliever, but it was convenient to do so and I wonder now whether or not my adoption of that attitude owed as much to laziness as to conviction. I say to the old man: 'You're an old hypocrite really, aren't you? You don't believe in any God.'

He looks at me, his eyes agape, but bright with the slither of new varnish. 'Are you sure that that is not a misconception of your youth?' he lisps.

141

'I remember it from childhood, yes.'

'The conceptions of a child are often false.'

I remember there was an old man whom we used to visit sometimes, not really very frequently, when I was quite small. He was a cousin of Mother's, I think. The recollection is sharp now. An old man with dirty stubble on his face; even his head was stubbled. He was a cripple and wore a grey woollen blanket about his legs as he sat in a large wooden armchair. He had on a grey pullover, just like Muller's, and wore old grey gloves. He was grey from head to foot. I can't recall any conversation that I ever had with him, and it is probable that he never spoke to me at any time, but I do remember him saying to Mother in an old grey voice: 'You should pray, my dear.' I don't know what preceded that remark. Mother used to pray, of course, and always attended church on Sunday mornings.

'Do you believe in God, then, old man?'

He is silent and I am silent. The wind is growing very chilly. I pull the remnants of my coat more closely around my shoulders.

'Not as a spirit in human form,' he says.

'I doubt if any thinking man really believes that any more.'

'Oh yes, yes they do.'

'You don't think that man is made in God's image, then?'

He snorts. 'Man makes God in his image; that is unforgivable vanity.'

'Well, how do you see God?'

'God is the summation of all man's thoughts. It is the coalescence of all the articulation, the dreams, the despairs and the agonies of all men. It is what man doesn't know, but recognises that there is to know. All that is God.'

'How, then, can we know God?'

'If we know something, it can hardly be divine.'

'Then God is the sum of man's ignorance.'

'Yes, of course. But man's dreams are made of his ignorance.'

'And before man?'

'God is man's concept. A concept cannot be without a mind

142

to conceive it.'

'I knew you didn't believe in God, Muller. That was not a misconception of my youth.'

'Listen to me, my son.' That phrase, echoing and re-echoing back down the years to the classroom. 'Listen to me, my son.' And I listened and I heard and I thought I understood. Now I see that understanding can never be final. It is not easy to give wisdom with words, although words can sit, they can distort and writhe and hurt, and return to shape in later times with later caution and then start to be wisdom. 'You have elected to be glib, when to reflect would gain so much more. I said that God is the summation of all man's thoughts. I said it was what his dreams are made of. I believe absolutely in the dreams of men. Dreams are the source of strength, of purpose. Ambition is a dream; love is a dream; tomorrow is a dream.'

'Is God simply a dreaming, then? Is religion nothing but dreaming?'

'Yes. Organised dreaming, of course, and because man's dreams are so different, so must the ethics and mechanics of religions be different. But God remains a dream. I do believe in that dream. I find that idea so much more acceptable, and so much more beautiful than the traditional one.'

Mother would take us to church with her on Sunday mornings. We would be scrubbed and brushed and stiffly groomed, then marched in a line behind her, jerking along like wooden toys. I suppose that was the beginning of disenchantment. Then into the hushed and awful gloom of the church, a place of polished pews and coloured glass and the odour of religion seeping from the very woodwork. It was a place where tyrants would smile, pale smiles of teeth and tightened skin with the eyes as cold as the coloured glass; where friends and kindly folk would frown, and where to be a child was a form of sin. I could never see the purpose of this falseness, as if people were trying to deceive the God they set out to worship, as though their God would assess them on the veneer he saw on a Sunday morning. So I have carried my own prejudice from those times that a church was a place where people behaved falsely; where they stood or knelt in formal, unnatural and uncomfortable postures, in formal, unnatural and uncomfortable stillness, where to shift position or scratch or even sniffle was a weakness beyond excuse. So one stood, one's ankles aching with restrained restlessness, an itch on one's bum that grew and tickled and demanded the delight of scratching, and one's nose tickling and filling and twitching in torment. All for an attitude. God was a Sunday attitude; he was discomfort and fear and unpleasantness, and I found it difficult not to reject him. But in later years my reason told me that I couldn't reject a concept, especially the concept of this God, because of the irrational practice of it. I don't know now that I do, but I prefer Muller's interpretation. He is, after all, just the voice of my own communion.

'Muller, how do I pray to a dream?'

'Prayers are dreaming. What are your dreams?'

'I have none now. I'm afraid to hope.'

'Is your island still there?'

'Oh yes, but I haven't heard any music for many days.'

'There has been no wind until today, no waves on the beach.'

'Waves on the beach are irrelevant. It must be that there's been no wind.'

*   *   *

I swam out to Reef Four today. It took considerable determination, not only because the weather is not at all pleasant – a very reluctant sun in a folded grimy sky, and the sea chopping listlessly – but also because of my own changed feelings about the place. Reef Four has affected me like the death of love. I have lost the capacity for enchantment, I cannot enjoy, for joy has deserted me.

The reef reflected my feelings; it, too, was joyless, dispirited. The water was cloudy with suspended organisms; there was no colour, and little movement in the grottoes and the weed. I kept looking skyward in ridiculous, mindless apprehension. I forced myself to stay there, to swim around and look, but even now I'm unsure of my exact motive. At length I swam back to the closer reefs. There was no current at all today, but I still feel tired. That is a symptom of my apathy. I see that I can't create pleasure, I can't synthesise hope. Yet I've lost too many hours in lethargy and that is an insidious form of mental wilt. I don't mind death, but I won't accept the erosion of my mind. That is my determination. That is my substitute for hope.

Writing is difficult now, with little room left in the book and the pencils very short, but I should do it for a record, for a purpose, and for the crystallisation of my thoughts.

My resolution has been stimulated by the madness of last night. It was a lapse into a new insanity, a conquest of the unconscious over the rational. I cannot let that happen, not again. There was Monique as well as Deirdre dancing on the beach, on the water, out to sea, circling back – two schoolgirls with pigtails and tutus and pink dancing shoes. It was a party and we had wine and cake and roast sucking pig with an apple in its mouth. There were paper hats and fairy lights, and there were crowds of people, faceless nameless people, all laughing and dancing and relentless, and they wouldn't go. I was unable to stand the noise. I couldn't hear the music. And Monique and Deirdre kept dancing and dancing, separate but in unison. I called out: 'Be quiet, be quiet, be quiet!' But the noise went on, louder and louder, pressing on me, hurting and hurting. Laughter all around me, mad laughter, nothing but laughter. Enfolding me. Smothering me. I flung out my arms and burst out of it. Suddenly silence. No persons and no noise. I walked down the beach towards the girls, towards the impossible vision of Monique in a tutu; but they were dancing out to sea, growing smaller and smaller, not hearing me, not seeing me. I stood open-armed on the beach. Imploring. But they didn't come.

It happened in wakefulness. It was not a dream. I am not concerned about dreams. I can only call it madness. So although there is no hope, there can never be hope again, still there is this purpose. The purpose of sanity. Writing must be part of that purpose. I am a hideous caricature of a man, but I will remain a sane one. I will never give up my mind.

*   *   *

My penknife has finally broken, parting at the brass pivot, but it has lasted far longer than I had considered likely, even though I've taken great care with it, using the edges of shells to cut with, in preference to the knife, whenever possible. In fact, the edges of shells are more serviceable for most functions, being sturdier and easier to grip. But the blade of the knife is sharper. I'd find it very difficult to sharpen my stubs of pencils, for instance, with a shell. I'll have to salvage it for that purpose, actually; either find some other way to hold the blade to the handle or fit the blade to a stick. I was using the penknife for the final shaping of a new face mask when it broke. This will be my third mask; continual immersion does make the fibres of the husks too soft and loose after a while. The knife was ideal for the detailed paring of the fibres essential for a perfect fit and for sealing the lenses initially; later the lenses actually seal better as the fibres swell. So it is vital to devise a way to hold the blade firmly. The challenge of a new invention will in itself be a benefit. I need challenges to fuel my purpose.

The menace of insanity is like a warder, restricting my freedom of mind. To maintain that the mind cannot be restricted, that physical imprisonment still allows the mind to reach out to heights and limits unknown, is a fallacy. Man's mind must have controls, it must have discipline, and in solitary confinement the degree of control becomes vital, for if the mind travels to the strange reaches of unchained imagination there is no one to guide its return to reality. Freedom of thought is a luxury of ordered society.

'All freedom is a luxury.' He is small and withered, huddled in his nightshirt.

'It most certainly isn't a right as is often expressed.'

'But it should be. Man is born free.' He is a prisoner, of

146

course, as much a prisoner as I; a captive of his own platitudes.

I scorn him. 'What utter rubbish! Man is born into a society, and immediately the constraints of that society limit his freedom. There is discipline, parental discipline, school discipline, the laws of the land, the stronger laws of social custom. Where is the freedom'

His head juts and droops from his nightshirt like a turtle's. He slobbers: 'Freedom is a matter of degree. There are only little freedoms within a great prison of social structures.' He pauses. He really looks tired and ill today. I wonder what he died of.

'Whatever state man is born into, it certainly isn't freedom,' I tell him. 'Just little freedoms, as you say, that emerge from the social order, like visits to Reef Four on this blasted island. So freedom is a myth because of social constraints. I don't have those here, so I can consider myself free. There are no policemen here, no laws; I can do whatever I like whenever it pleases me, within the limitations imposed by range. Tell me, is that more freedom than other men enjoy?'

'Do you enjoy it?'

'The limitation of range is one of the most severe. I would give anything to be able to wander unbounded for one hour, just one hour with a constant change of scene and surroundings. Oh yes, that would be a freedom. All I see, day after interminable day, is this hateful sea, the same hateful circle of beach and a handful of trees. Just to be able to walk far enough away not to see any of that, even for a few minutes. To get out of this damnable cell, to extend my range, that would be worth all the so-called social constraints. If only I could reach that other island.'

'Your constraints are only physical. Surely social ones could be more restrictive, such as actual imprisonment.'

'Even imprisonment is a social condition. I have the restrictions without the human contact. I wouldn't want prison, but otherwise I could willingly sacrifice freedom of action, even freedom of thought, for the single benefit of company; though in all honesty I would have rejected such a thought

147

when I was part of a social condition. There's nothing quite like complete absence of so-called rights or benefits to make one appreciate them.'

The sun is orange, sinking into the quicksand of purple cloud, gold rimmed on the horizon. The sea is violet in the dusk. I hear the soft lap of an undecided tide; I wait for the music, but there is none. Apart from the kiss of the water on the beach, everything is still. Muller is vague and grey, just an unclear bundle propped close by. He mutters vaguely and dimly like his intrusion into the evening: 'Does one have any rights? Benefits deriving from a commitment to society, certainly, but not rights. Rights are a myth.'

The night has set now. It's quite black close to me; further out the sea still glimmers in a limited starlight. There must be a breeze, for the first faint notes of music are reaching me. I have to peer at these pages to write, but I feel reluctant to stop.

'It is the mighty alone who have rights.' The words of the old man never intrude upon my writing. He waits until I'm ready.

'I'm not concerned with rights. All I want is some company, and some variety in my environment.' I pause, wondering if he has left me, but there is still a shadowed form there. 'You aren't company, Muller. Your thoughts are my thoughts; your arguments are my arguments. I need another mind to duel with.'

I can see lights now from the other place, and hear the sounds of revelry above the music. How can I get there? Some men could swim that distance. Men have swum further, and I am extraordinarily fit; my left hand is a bit deformed now, but it's only a slight inconvenience when swimming. No, it's a crazy thought. I couldn't even see the island from the surface of the sea and would have no idea of direction. There would be sharks, too. But really it is just too far. It is a long, long way and I simply couldn't swim that distance.

'And you're not even sure it's there.'

'Oh, go away, Muller.'

＊　　＊　　＊

148

Muller was not my only teacher and, upon reflection, was probably not the most important one. I can't explain why my mind has selected him as a projection for my ruminations, but I suppose he is the product of the indelible attitudes impressed on a greening mind. He isn't the truth of Muller, I understand that; he is a composite of several mentors of whom he was probably the closest to an archetype. A man of banality, because the banal was required as a foundation for inspiration, but as I remember him, one who did encourage those stumbling thoughts beyond the banal; perhaps mistaken thoughts, probably too quickly conceived, but thoughts that reached out for something above the layered platitudes of the classroom. That might not have been Muller, though; perhaps Dawkins or Mrs Downham, or Foster. No, not Foster, but somewhere in that fusty group was the unclosed mind that refused to latch the minds of youth. The banality was undoubtedly necessary, but education owes more to that other factor and the teacher who understood it.

As far as I can recall, Muller was never my form master. He taught mathematics and science theory, I think, but only in my early years of adolescence. I must have liked him, though no particular affinity with any of the teachers in my puberty comes to mind. Now I come to think of it, I don't remember Muller ever wearing a mortarboard or gown; he always wore a navy-blue suit, severely pressed, with a waistcoat and a tie; he was a very clean man, very spruce, and I'm sure that he shaved every morning. The nightshirt, the stubble, the lisp in his voice, are attributes from my own garbled memories, reflecting a sort of mental symbolism, I suppose.

It was Foster who wore a mortarboard and gown. He was my form master when I first went to secondary school; a history teacher, an erudite and most unbending man. I think it's only his attire and possibly his stance that my composite wraith has adopted. But Foster was a very clever man, so learned that he rarely referred to a textbook in his teaching, but never, never wrong. His cleverness was in his admirable memory; he wouldn't forget a single fact once he had read it, nor would he get a quotation wrong, and he was strong on quotations. He was an inexhaustible store of information, and we schoolchildren stood in awe of him. Yet I see now that his vast erudition was the erudition of others, learned well and understood well, but not added to, altered or developed in any way. Foster wasn't capable of originality, of insight, or of wisdom. He didn't need it; he was infallibly secure in an extensive wisdom of others. He instilled in us, or endeavoured to, and I think with much success, the love of knowledge. For him it was enough just to know, and this must have made him an excellent teacher; those who followed his way would be excellent citizens, conformists secure in the absolute confidence of their rightness. But on Foster's path, there could be no extension of knowledge, no new theories, just a library of the already known; a vast library, almost infinite, for there is a lot of learning to be done – one can learn forever. Foster and the disciples of Foster – and I'm sure there were many of them – were devoted to learning, but could never, *would* never, contribute to that learning.

We never had a dais in our secondary school classroom. That image I have retained, of a large desk and a raised platform, must be from an earlier year of my education. There was a man with a gown in that classroom, but it wasn't Muller. I can't give that teacher a name, but I do remember Mrs Downham on the dais. I adored Mrs Downham. She was tall and hung with corners; thin square shoulders, sharp elbows, projecting knees, even her hipbones jutted out as if her skirt was draped on a coathanger; but she was a lovely woman. I don't know what she actually taught us, probably most of what we had to learn in those early years; she was in the classroom more often than the man. But I do remember her compassion, and her red hair; it was a startling colour, dyed I would think, and piled high on her head, making her seem even taller than her natural height. But mainly I remember her compassion. She must have loved children; she seemed to have enough love for her whole class. She would often cuddle us, all of us, I think – there was no favouritism that I recall – and gently help us with our

150

problems with an arm around a little shoulder and quiet encouraging words, and perhaps a kiss as she stood up and moved on to the next child. That's how I remember her, anyway, and it's a picture that I have no wish to erase with some other doubtful truth; though now, from the scarred, cynical mentality of my adulthood, I see that we children were her substitute family, filling the void within her of the children she never had. Still, I reject even that thought as unkind, unfair and unnecessary. I shall preserve the memory of Mrs Downham as I believe I knew her, as I experienced her, as a person of warmth and tenderness, of gentle words in my ear and of making me want to do it right so that she would be pleased. The causes of her kindness are irrelevant and I don't care about them. She was a lovely woman and I did adore her. That memory is intact and inviolate; the understanding of maturity will not soil it.

These are all the words I have written in a month, although the time period is but a guess; I have given up recording the days on the sand. Writing is difficult and I've only written today because I've been holed up in my shelter for nearly two days. No rain, just a terrible wind. More coconuts have fallen; I hope the whole crop won't be destroyed again. But I have enjoyed the writing and the reminiscing, although it's really an extravagance in terms of my remaining potential for recording anything. There isn't much pencil left and very little space in the book. My writing is getting smaller and smaller; soon it will be impossible to read. But I doubt if anyone will ever read it.

*　　*　　*

I am determined to swim round the island. The total distance is estimated at about a mile which should be well within my capacity. I don't go to Reef Four any more, although I often plan a swim there. Somehow I'm reticent. But this swim round the island is something I've thought about for several days, not commencing it, so that I could savour the planning. There are almost certainly parts of the shoreline in whose waters I haven't yet swum, although I don't expect any unusual revelations. The unexpected will likely be currents and rips, particularly in the southern area which is less familiar to me. I'll keep to within a few yards of the shore in case my courage falters for any reason – the sight of a shark, too strong a rip or just plain tiredness. This will be the first time.

It's evening now and the swim is over. It was really very easy; the distance wasn't at all arduous and there were no alarms. Tomorrow I'll do it again, but further out. A few yards further from shore could almost double the distance.

'You're not in training, are you?'

'Of course not. Training for what?'

*   *   *

My city is complete. It has occupied me for four days. I swim in the mornings, at least once round the island and then some more. Soon I'll be doing two circuits. In the afternoons I have been building my city. It is made of sand which has to be moistened to give it some stability. Coconut shells form my mould, and there are multitudes of sea shells as decoration; these also aid the support of the sand once the moisture evaporates, otherwise the material collapses. It is a sand castle, nothing more, but a magnificent sand castle, with a palace and a cathedral and railway stations, with an aerodrome and schools and a hospital; it has streets and cars and people; it has a lake and a forest, and above those a mountain. I sit and look at it. This is my creation and it gives me a great deal of pleasure. Especially at night with the moon donating its silver, and the glints of the shells, and the shadows shaping the mounds and the clefts. It is an enchantment, a magic city.

But the first rain will destroy it. It is doomed as Sodom was doomed. As I am doomed.

*   *   *

This morning I swam three times round the island. That must be at least five miles. I was very, very tired but I wasn't exhausted. I had not reached my limits. I can swim five miles. Five miles.

✻   ✻   ✻

The clouds are painted on the sky. It is an unmoving day. The sea has been planed flat and shimmers like a sheet of steel. I lie just as motionless within my citadel, and my spider, who has no habit of motion, sits and waits out his eternal vigil, ready for some foolish, impossible bluebottle to stumble into his snare. The sun glares down. Everything waits in unrecognised, un-recorded time. What will happen when the waiting is over? Will movement occur when the sun removes its wrath to some other quarter? Is everything just waiting for darkness? Surely the night will be less pitiless, the cool will stir the air, the moon will move the sea. I am tempted to swim again just to disturb the water. It would be an empty gesture, though, my puny ripples would be nothing but a momentary violation and would serve no purpose, even to my own vanity.

Even as I wrote those words something moved on the surface, a mere few yards from where I sit. It is a turtle. Now I *will* go swimming.

I wrestled with the turtle in the sea but it was too strong for me, and I lost it. Yet, for a minute, perhaps two, but no more than that, there was an excitement. It was a new sort of thrill for me and one at which my sophisticated nature should be appalled, born of instincts formed long before sophistication was a factor in human make-up, instincts that cultured man caters for in his aggressive sports – boxing, hunting, fighting bulls – or by just observing others doing such things. But the participation itself is the thrill of the hunting beast, a naked, wild thrill, and as such I recognised it and was intoxicated by it, heightened as it was by the rarity of any form of excitement. I lost the turtle, but the struggle has satisfied the savagery of a heritage close to the primal but etched into my soul by a later evolution. I am deeply satisfied. The island can still offer something.

Otherwise the day has not moved.

☆   ☆   ☆

I am very tired.

Editor's Note
These words, 'I am very tired', were written on the corner of one page, unassociated with other writing on that page. It is not possible to vouch without qualification for the accurate determination of their position in the general narrative, particularly as the content of the single short sentence is open to more than one interpretation. I was tempted to omit it, but the criterion of authenticity decided its inclusion.

The backs of my hands are very brown. When I move my fingers the skin piles up in little ridges, like a wind-ruffled pool. They look like old hands, the old hands of an Indian farmer. Not only my hands but my whole body is extraordinarily brown. I have a brown penis. But it isn't the pleasant brown of naturally brown-skinned people, it has no lustre at all. It is the sere, harsh brown of unnatural exposure, a dry brown like the skin of a snake, lacking in smoothness and lacking in the sheen of health. I suffer much from blisters on the lips and a flaking nose. It is strange how the races of the sun have large lips and broad noses, and yet they rarely suffer from such solar effects.

Races aren't the same, in spite of the claims of some idealists.

'That's a racist sentiment,' intones Muller, parading the classroom floor in his nightshirt.

'Maybe so. If it offends, I am sorry, but I can't say otherwise for that reason.'

'All men are of the same species.' He has stopped parading momentarily, in order to make that statement with emphasis.

'All dogs are dogs,' I respond, 'but they're not all alike.'

'Likeness isn't any sort of criterion.'

'For what?'

'For judgement of race.'

'Ah, but I'm making no judgements. I'm in no way assessing worth, any more than I would assess worth between a sheep-dog and a St Bernard. Their merits are measured under totally different standards. My statement, that you termed racist, in fact gives dark-skinned peoples an advantage over us Europeans; they are better able to withstand exposure to the sun – that is incontestable, but it's a matter of specific evolution only.'

Muller wanders up and down with surprising vigour for one so shrivelled. 'This is an argument for racial purity,' he screeches, taut with feeling.

'No, no, not for racial purity at all; racial recognition, perhaps.'

I remember a black boy in my class at primary school. He was an extremely popular individual although he never did well at lessons. We called him 'Sambo', with a certain naive cruelty, although I don't recall an instance when he showed the slightest offence; perhaps that developed in later years. Actually I know his name was Daniel. In our play, the only effect his colour had on us was one of identification. He was one of us, the same as us, no better or worse at games than the average boy. He was popular because he liked fun, and he laughed at anything, no matter how unfunny, if it was presented as humour. He enjoyed laughter for its own sake. There was a time, too short, really, when I was especially close to him. But now I don't know what became of him. I think he left our district long before the end of our primary school years, and with the temporariness of childhood affection he was soon replaced in my particular ambit.

Daniel's colouring was, in fact, no darker than mine at the present time. I doubt if he would be any fitter to survive in the jungles of his ancestral land than I, raised as he was in an English environment, nor stronger, nor cleverer, and yet to no degree less so. He would suffer less from sunburn, I suppose; that would be our only fundamental difference.

'More than that, I think,' says Muller. He is still with me, squatting now, his back against a palm tree.

'Now who is making racist remarks?'

'There is no point in an untruth to serve an ideal, as you've already remarked,' he replies. 'But there are certain impressions on man's heritage of soul that are racially characteristic. More recent, perhaps, than the ancient stamp of fire, possibly only barely scratched into the genetic substance, but enough to produce racial identity beyond simple physical properties of skin and lips.'

'You mean voodoo?'

Muller shudders. 'Heaven forbid. Nothing so dramatic. Certain musical inclinations, perhaps; responses to particular rhythms in speech and song; even responses to phases of the sun and moon that develop from the various latitudes of racial evolvement. They aren't so deep, these aspects, as the more primitive responses like fear of the dark, but they are apparent and have been documented.'

Muller may be right, but to me, here and now, all that matters is that my lips get blistered.

I shall leave Muller to his reflections and proceed with my latest occupational project. These days I don't berate myself for belated inspiration. I am resigned to my lack of natural invention even though this current project may have been the most obvious one of all. One has seen it portrayed countless times in picture shows, comics, even in the cartoons that so often caricature a circumstance close to mine. An SOS on the beach. Large letters that can be easily seen from the air. If ever a 'plane comes this way again. I have no hope. It isn't hope that drives me, more the determination to have done everything that could have been done to effect a rescue. There can never really be hope again.

My city has eroded back to even beach, more by wind and

drying sun than by the action of the sea. It is there that I have begun my letters. I use shells, selected ones that are darker than the white of the beach, and although there are many such shells, they are small, mostly smaller than a fingernail, and it needs several hundred to make a letter just three feet long. It was my original intention to make them two or three times that length, but that would take a long time. I have abundant time, but in the interim a smaller message is better than none at all. I can always extend the letters as time goes by. I have only the last S to do.

*   *   *

Gradually I have reverted to a diurnal existence, although the nights are still times for wandering on the dappled beach and washing in the music of the other place. But usually I fall asleep. I awoke last night and it was dark, as close to utter darkness as I have experienced. I was within the shelter. Outside there was no moon at all and only one star faint in the north. Somehow it was enjoyable. I folded the darkness about me and lay still.

I had awoken thinking of Daniel, the boy we called 'Sambo'. There's a puzzle here. I liked Daniel. All the children liked him, even Snotty Wilson. There was absolutely no animosity, racial or otherwise, for Daniel and, in our innocence, no conception that there could have been. I'm not sure whether it was the same with the teachers, although Mrs Downham cuddled him just like the rest of us. I was convinced as I lay in the darkness that racial animosity is not a thing of instinct. The puzzle is, why do we feel any such animosity as adults, and then convince ourselves that it's a natural reaction? And then, by some strange twist of logic, instruct ourselves that the reaction is wrong? Of course it's wrong. But the reaction occurs, whether it's an induced one or a natural one.

'Undoubtedly an induced one,' said a voice, firm from the night. I saw nobody. Now, as I write some hours later, I shan't record that it was the voice of Muller. The identity is unim-

157

portant. It was a projected thing from which to rebound my thoughts.

'Why do we have this racial hostility? If it isn't natural, why do we induce it?'

'The reasons are historical,' intoned the voice. 'Invasion of the lands of another race automatically makes them the enemy. Add to that the superiority of Caucasian technology, then slavery, and then the various concepts of beauty, and you have the seeds of prejudice.'

'Prejudice, yes. But I'm not satisfied that prejudice necessarily equates with hostility. Invasion equates with hostility, that is clear, but that applies regardless of race. Invasion didn't always occur with other races; probably rarely so, actually, in the total history of warfare.'

Yet somehow the factor of invasion did seem, for me lying entombed in the dark, to be the key to the puzzle. Man invades man for many token reasons: he needs the other's food, the other's water, the other's minerals, maybe even the other's women; although one can't help postulating that trading might have achieved the same ends. But there's another, deeper-seated reason for invasion. It is simply that man needs to invade. He's an aggressive creature; he needs to have 'enemy'. Man creates 'enemy'. That need is close to the primal heritage, close to the beginning of voracious life. The concept of 'enemy' is as basic to living matter as survival itself. In the urban savagery, where hostility is current – always realised but rarely comprehended – the need of 'enemy' manifests itself in many ways. Ganghood and the factor of territory are the most readily recognised, but in the search for a culprit for the known hostility, which is indeed nothing but the need for 'enemy', a stranger, any stranger, can fulfil the role. But 'stranger' is too often identified with 'strangeness'. There lies the essence of racial animosity. It is unreasonable, it is unjust and it is bigoted, but it is part of the nature of man, part of the nature of life itself.

'That's an apology for racism,' responded the voice.

'Yes, sadly, that is all one can do. Apologise.'

I must have fallen asleep again after that. It had been a hard day before. The last S is finished. There was an added benefit in the search for shells yesterday. I found a bird, a dead bird, being washed onto the beach by the tide, reminding me of a mother urging a reluctant child into the bathroom. I picked it up, at first with but a mild interest, when it dawned on me that a bird has feathers, and pillows can be made of feathers. So today I'll start to make a pillow using what remains of my singlet. I'll need more feathers than those off one bird. Now there is a positive reason for catching them. My previous attempts have all met with failure but there was never a great deal of incentive for exercising my ingenuity. Surely an educated mind should be able to think of something. Now, many months since my arrival, the possibility of a minor degree of comfort is like the promise of a hot bath after a day's work in the fields. An unimaginable luxury.

※　　※　　※

I've been attempting to catch the damn' birds for a week. Well, at least I have established a possible method, but it needs perfecting. The birds will eat fish offal, excitedly and enthusiastically, on the open sand, but it is futile to place it under cover as I did with my initial attempts using my coat. They just won't enter any form of enclosure; perhaps free flying birds, as these are, have an inbuilt suspicion of closed spaces. When I tried casting the bait into a loop of ribbon, I found that the exposed ribbon was treated as warily as my coat. So I covered the ribbon with a dusting of sand. Once again the birds showed an enthusiasm for taking the offal, but unfortunately they were far too swift. I had no chance to retreat to hiding in order to spring the trap, and on the only occasion I managed to snatch the ribbon while a bird was within the loop, the loop didn't close, and even if it had, the bird would already have been feet into the air.

The birds have gone now; they are far from daily visitors, but they will come back. I've worked out a refinement of the basic trap. It will be necessary to place the offal in a depression with the ribbon concealed at the rim, and staked so that the loop will close when I pull the tail. The birds will have to fly into the hollow to retrieve the bait, giving me an extra second to make my move. In order to encourage a feeding frenzy, I shall cast bits of offal at them from a distance. Sooner or later a piece will fall into the depression and hopefully an excited bird will swoop onto it. That's my plan. All I have to do is wait for the birds' return. One bird's feathers make a frugal pillow. Nevertheless I am thankful for it.

❊   ❊   ❊

I have had a fall. I fell about twenty feet, and although not badly hurt, I'm shaking so badly that it isn't easy to write. There are a few abrasions and a massive bruise on one ankle, but I can walk; the trembling of my legs is only the reaction of battered nerves. The injuries are only the smallest part of the tragedy. I have killed my spider. That is a pain far greater than the throbbing of an ankle. My sole companion is dead. He was my only friend in this alien hell, and I have crushed him. He has been splattered into oblivion. All that is left are two legs held together by a scrap of yellow. The web, the beautiful web, remains as gossamer threads. And to me all blame must attach. I feel a guilt, a self-treachery when I believed that here there could be no such concept as guilt. To destroy this life, to destroy my one companion, my one real existing, breathing, vibrant companion, was an act of senseless murder.

The pegs in the trunks of the palm trees have dried and withered in the sun. I knew that when I began to climb. One broke off at the very start. I chose to ignore the warning. I wanted a coconut and felt that by keeping my feet close in to the trunk the pegs would take the strain. They did, although again one cracked near the top. I was then too close to the coconuts to desist. Folly. Stupid, unforgivable folly. At the top it was necessary to reach out at full stretch to touch the nuts. The peg beneath my right foot snapped with complete, unwarned suddenness. For an instant I saw everything with an utter clarity. The coconuts just above my eyes; a palm frond offering a false stability; the trunk starting to move away and, beyond, the porcelain sea bearing the blueness of sky on its surface. That scene is sharp. Afterwards, only the alarm of falling, a brief second of incomprehension. Comprehension didn't come until the awareness that I had landed and was still intact. The shelter cushioned the fall. My feet went through the roof, skidding past a turtle shell and smashing unresistant palm fronds; my arse collided with one of the supporting boughs, dislodging it and crushing the spider against a rock. My buttocks are sore. The spider is dead.

So he has gone. I mourn with a grief out of proportion to the spider's size. I wonder if life *has* any size. A spider's life should really only have value to other spiders, and even that is probably untrue. Spiders are fundamentally a species content with aloneness. I identified him as a companion; he would not have viewed me in the same light. But my grief is also composed of my guilt; I have destroyed something very beautiful, and beauty here is a precious gift. I shall go on without him; I shall rebuild my shelter; nothing much will have changed. Except in me. A part of my belief, my reason for enduring, has gone with the spider. There is nothing left to love. One can't love a coconut tree.

*   *   *

I must get away from here.

*   *   *

Beyond Reef Four there are other reefs, much deeper, too deep for diving as I dive. There are fish of considerable size on those reefs, but not readily distinguished from the surface. I convinced myself that they weren't sharks. That conviction was necessary.

The sea was flat again this morning, so I decided to swim

straight out from the island. Above the flatness the palm trees marked the direction for my return. In the plain words of recording that decision I might be saying, in other circumstances, that I decided to stroll along a highway. The words of record don't report the apprehension that created an almost insuperable reluctance even to enter the water. My whole body had to be forced step by step through the application of a controlled will, across the beach and into the discouraging sea. Swimming around the island engendered no such reluctance; safety was then only minutes away. It was the knowledge today that, whatever time it took to swim out, it would take an equal time to return, which was part of my wilted spirit; it was the trepidation of known dangers and unknown dangers, the latter being the most dominant; it was the awesome vastness of the ocean and my total reliance on stable weather to ensure my orientation within that vastness; most of all, it was sheer, abject fear that trickled through me, through my veins and my sinews, and dripped into the yellow bile of terror. But I did it. I did it. And in doing it I have demonstrated a strength of purpose that has achieved an incalculable impetus for my self-esteem. It was a triumph. In other times and other places such a feat would be hardly worthy of comment; a man swims a mile out to sea and back again. A trivial thing. Men, and women, too, have swum the English Channel. What is a mere two miles measured against such a yardstick? But for me the sense of achievement, the elation felt, is as if I had indeed swum a channel. I have overcome more than the rigours of extreme fatigue, more than the resistance of strengthless muscles, more than the pain of agonised lungs. I have overcome fear, fear that had settled into every inch of my physical being, every molecule of my soul; my will alone remained to challenge it. And my will was victorious.

Actually the swim itself was, in the physical sense, of no duress at all. There were no wild currents to contend with, no chop on the water; I might have been idly exercising in a swimming pool if it weren't that there was at least something to view. Not much; a few deep reefs and a distant sea bed, sometimes too deep still to reflect an image. I held direction by maintaining a set distance between two selected palms. The actual swimming was easy, even enjoyable. I feel no more than a pleasant tiredness, as one might after a friendly game of tennis, not extended and still ready for other activity. But I won the game, and my mental state is that of a conqueror.

'What was the object of the exercise?'

'Does it matter? Only the achievement matters. I've beaten the phantoms. I feel the return of arrogance and I like the sensation. It is good.'

'What if you had seen a shark, just one little shark?'

Muller is right. I know that the sight of a single shark would have defeated me. 'But that would not have been the phantoms, old man. That would have been a real and tangible danger.'

'And next time?'

'Next time a shark will fill me with caution but not alarm, not panic. I have control over my reactions. Today a shark would have beaten my will. Tomorrow it won't. Never again.'

'Will you do it again?'

'Why not?'

'It appears to have no purpose.' He is taller today. Taller and straighter, and his lisp is hardly noticeable. I can't see his face for he's looking out to sea.

'Nothing has much purpose here.'

'Only survival, perhaps.'

'Perhaps. Even that is debatable. But I have achieved survival. All my other activities are for amusement only.'

He looks at me and he has the face of my father. Two halves of a face sewn together by a strip of hair; eyes so kind and worried. He says: 'Look after yourself, my boy. Take care.' And he goes.

I am deeply moved by this vision of my father. It is a manifestation that evades my reasoning. I want to cry. There is some emotion so deep, so connected with the early bonds of infancy; so invoking of images, of arms reaching out for reassurance, small fingers grasping a large and strong one, and

163

the touch is a current of trust and security; so filling that the fullness is a void of bewilderment; an emotion so enmeshed in the essence of myself and so long buried that I am shattered. My arrogance is shattered. I can't cry. I've forgotten how to cry. The darkness is coming. The darkness is coming.

Editor's Note
This last paragraph was an exceptionally disjointed piece of writing. Perhaps because he was very moved, but also because his remaining blank space was very limited. Even the duplication of the last sentence may not have been intentional. He wrote it twice, but the first time is so blurred I believe it was done with lead worn down to the wood of the pencil. Later he must have sharpened it and rewritten the words; it's difficult to guess his motive. It is the last writing on that page – nothing else could have been coherently fitted in.

Swam four times around the island today. The sea was dark and choppy; getting worse now, though I don't know why. The wind isn't especially strong. I am exhausted; in that sea I must have reached close to my limits. But I swam at least six miles, maybe seven.

*　　*　　*

There was a bit of rain, thunder far away, but now the sea has settled. Underneath the grey surface it is murky and un-pleasant. I collected some sea-urchins and a large empty shell shaped like a bugle. I have knocked the tip off but can't make it produce any reasonable sound. It has several holes piercing its external surface, though, so perhaps if I can patch those it could still be used as a trumpet. I would need some glue. What can I use for glue? If I remember correctly, the adhesive that we used in our woodwork classes at school was made of powdered fishbone. I have plenty of fishbone and powdering it doesn't present a problem. Boiling it up, however, won't be a simple matter, although I only need a little fire for the minute quantity of glue required; there would be enough in a shell the size of a bottle cap.

✳   ✳   ✳

My bugle works, although its sound is more like a bass trumpet, and it has taken me three days of continuous practice to acquire any degree of consistency at all, and it will take much longer to produce anything that could be called a tune. Nevertheless, I'm delighted with it. I patched the holes successfully, sticking broken bits of shell over them; the glue works amazingly well. Actually, I thought I heard a responsive sound from the other island last evening. Could they have heard me?

'It was an echo,' says the stupid old man.

'Nonsense,' I tell him.

Tonight I'll climb a coconut tree and blast away from the top.

The evening is quite beautiful. From the top of the tree the sky seemed like a shroud between the world and darkness, far, far away; the sea was a twitching surface, more metallic than in the liquid daylight, bouncing and breaking the light from the moon; the moon itself was shy, peeping and winking and sidling behind the clouds. I blew a most glorious, single enduring note from the trumpet, like the scream of a falling man. And I waited. I couldn't see the island – no lights, no bulk of dark shadow. There was no music, no wind, no chance of echo. For a long time there was only silence. It was an incredible silence on the top of that tree, with the strangeness of a new vision of night all about me. Almost a beautiful silence, except that I was waiting with too much expectancy. And then it came. It could not be mistaken for an echo. The sound was different, the note was different, the duration was even longer than my own. It could only be a response to my call. I blew again. And again the response. They hear me; they know I'm here.

It is unbelievable, but my waiting is over. My sojourn here is near its end. Oh God, I believe in you. I believe in you.

＊ ＊ ＊

Still they haven't come. Three days and still they haven't come.

＊ ＊ ＊

Why don't they come? Every night I blow the trumpet, but now the wind is in the wrong direction and they can't possibly hear me. It must be that they do not understand my predicament. Is it possible to send a message by bugle? I don't know the morse code, even if the wind were blowing the right way. I think SOS is three long and three short blasts, then three long blasts again. Later I shall try that, anyway, as soon as the wind is right. I can wait. It's only a matter of time, after all, a bit more time than I had anticipated, but a few more days cannot matter. I know they will come eventually.

＊ ＊ ＊

I crawled up the beach without even strength to stand. I lost count of the circuits – at least six. I just kept swimming and swimming until my arms refused to move. It was a swim of desperation but my despair is still with me. Twenty-two days now since I first made a bugle call; a week since I began my repetitious SOS blasts. They still respond, but they don't come.

There isn't much more space anywhere in this book, neither have I much pencil left, but it will outlast the space. What shall

166

I do with it? If they don't come, how shall I get my chronicle to the world? But they will come. I'm sure they'll come.

*   *   *

I want to die. Now I do want to die. The bugle is smashed. It is in a dozen pieces; there is no way it can be repaired. I had it tied to my belt while I climbed a tree for the evening call. And it fell. It slipped out of the loop and hit the shelter. They haven't come, and if they don't hear my call they will forget I am here. They'll think I was a passing boat.

I sit in a welter of wretchedness. How can I die?

*   *   *

I've scoured the reefs for another bugle shell, living or dead. They must be there, but I haven't found one. I haven't permitted myself to wade in this morass of self-pity for a long time; I've forgotten the technique to defeat it. But really it is the drive that is weak. I had built myself something of a substitute life, and while hope was kept intentionally dormant, I was able to make it, I could manage to endure. I created my rituals, from daily swims to rain dances; I created projects to absorb my mind; I talked to a wraith, and the talking and the projects somehow filled the blankness of this non-existence. Now I haven't the drive even to care. It rained, but I didn't dance. Muller hasn't come again and I don't want him. Hope has been exposed, brought roaring into vibrant life, overtaking and swamping my pitiful inventions, obliterating them beyond an easy recovery. And now, with that hope dying, a void remains where before were my artifices. Hope hasn't finally gone yet, not altogether. I still stare out at the sea watching for the boat, but that really is as much the welling despair as it is the fading hope.

Those must be almost my last words. Only the top half of the cover is left – I used the bottom half to light a fire for my glue. So this is the end. I must save the journal. Whatever happens I must save the journal. My substance is in these pages. Someone will find it. The world will not forget me.

It is evening now. A dark and still time. But the music is clear. The other place is not too far away. It's not too far away.

EPILOGUE

The skipper of the *Sea Lord III*, one Dave Hartley, was a most methodical man. He had divided our search area up into squares on his charts and we ranged each section as systematically as the randomness of islands permitted. Our island was probably an uncharted one anyway, so certainly no blame attaches to him that, in the event, our six-month expedition proved inconclusive. He gave the utmost possible value for our money, and just a little more.

Denis, our skipper on the *Galathea*, had certainly exaggerated when he told us that there were thousands of islands and atolls in the South Pacific, but they must surely number in the hundreds. We explored the Ellice Island group, the Gilbert Islands, the Phoenix Islands, the Friendly Islands, the Society Islands and great distances of ocean in between. There were so many isolated islets and atolls that I lost count of the number we visited, although it is true that we only bothered to explore a few of them. We numbered those that we covered – there were thirty-one. Obviously we were able to eliminate those in a group easily visible from each other; nor did we bother with true coral atolls – we weren't looking for a coral atoll; nor islands with exposed coral reefs, nor islands of reef material – ours was certainly not a coral island. We also kept clear of islands within normal shipping lanes. Yet still there remained a large number of possibilities to be eliminated from our list one by one. Some had high hills, or were covered too thickly in vegetation; some had lagoons and some had springs of fresh water. So, as time passed and the list of eliminations grew long, our time and resources grew short.

We had allowed two weeks for our return trip. That date

finally came. It was a day of storm and choppy seas, not conducive to my personal well-being, for I had discovered that in such conditions I am really not a very good sailor. By this time my sea legs were sufficiently well developed so that I wasn't exactly ill, just feeling terrible, unhappy and coping with a headache. The imminent end of the trip did not strike me as too tragic at the time, although Val, on whom the sea had no apparent effect, was restless with her disappointment as we turned for home.

We were now in uncharted waters and, as was his practice in such circumstances, Dave Hartley placed a watch in the bow that night. In the early hours of the morning, when the light was already grey and unexpected intrusions in the sea were readily visible, an island was spotted, one not shown on any charts. As we drew nearer, we saw that it was low and flat and that it had a single clump of coconut palms approximately in the centre. Our hopes rose, until we realised that the island was over a thousand yards long and almost as wide. It was far too big.

The rough sea was making me feel queasy and I had had enough. 'Let's go home,' I said, finally conceding defeat. Val squeezed my hand. She was as disappointed as I was. More, perhaps.

We disembarked in Cairns ten days overdue and not a little out of pocket. And still we were not sure.

* * *

I was heartily sick of islands and even more sick of boats. In this there was certainly something of *mal de mer*, but surely more of disappointment, the aftermath of hope defeated, irrespective of how forlorn had been that hope in the beginning. Yet still there was a lingering doubt, a suspicion that lay immobile on the mind so that whenever, during the weeks and months that followed, one relaxed, a persistent thought came again and again, no matter how hard one tried to shake it off: the thought that possibly more could have been done, more expanses of sea explored, more islets paced and measured.

'You know, it's all very unsatisfactory,' said Val one evening, as she typed the last few words of the Coconut Book from my longhand decipherment. She pulled the sheet from her typewriter and looked it over quickly for errors. 'He must be dead now, mustn't he?' she added. 'Without any doubt?'

'There's always a doubt, of course,' I answered. 'The possibility of a rescue at last can't be entirely ruled out. There was that SOS on the beach.'

'It's not what you really believe, though, is it?'

It certainly wasn't, nor is it now. One assumes that the coconut in which the book was found had been at sea for a year or two, judging by the decomposed state of the denim ribbon when we first hauled it from the sea. It is difficult for me to accept that the man survived, or even wished to survive, for very long at all once his single powerful link with sanity had gone. To suppose otherwise seems to me to refute all the evidence of the chronicle itself. The very fact that he consigned it to the sea would indicate some final intention, some deliberate and considered course of action that for some reason he was reluctant to write down. There was, indeed, still a modicum of blank space on the torn half of the back cover below his final words, in which he could well have expressed whatever may have been on his mind at the end. To my way of thinking, that blank space is as significant as any other clue that we have. He would not tell the world that he was surrendering to an illusion: that illusion of another island. That illusion was no more real to the inner core of rationality that he possessed than was Muller. He created it, and, just as he understood the fiction of Muller, so he would have realised the fiction of the island. In the innermost depths of his heart he knew it wasn't there, I am sure of that. But he was still determined to swim away as if it *was* there, in the pretence that it wouldn't be suicide. It was as if he was trying to convince other people of the actual presence of the island.

Predictably, my wife doesn't share this view. She is of the

opinion that he did believe in the truth of the other island, but conversely, that he would not have attempted to swim to it. Her views are as sound as mine, her reasoning just as plausible. If he did believe in the other island, then he would still have hoped for communication with it eventually. He had made some quite emphatic and unwavering statements on the horrors of drowning, so he would never elect to die in that way. 'His courage would have faltered, even if he did attempt it,' she claimed that evening. 'It would not have outlasted his strength. He would have turned back before he reached the point of no return. If he was going to leave the island for good, he would have built a raft. The trees would not have mattered any more.'

'Perhaps he did. Perhaps we should have looked for an island with no trees on it at all.'

Val considered that, looking at me pensively. 'How would he have fastened the logs together?' she asked at last.

We discussed the various possibilities open to him. There was obviously denim ribbon which, if several strands were twisted together, might have made a rope of adequate strength. He could have cut up his shirt and jacket to make more fastenings. Perhaps he could have made rope from coconut fibre or palm sinews.

Still, my conviction is that he would never have attempted such a thing. He would never have destroyed his trees. If that had been his intention, he would surely have recorded it. That blank space can say only one thing: 'I am now going to swim away. The island has defeated me!'

*   *   *

Yet there is a footnote to the story which could, perhaps, lead to a more positive conclusion. Almost two years after our expedition, I received a letter from Dave Hartley. It reads:

Dear Richard,

You were aware of my keen interest in your Coconut

Book, and you know that I was almost as disappointed as yourself in the failure of our expedition to locate the island. Since that time I have broadcast the story around in various parts of the Pacific, in the hope that seaman's gossip might jolt someone's memory. I had in mind that there had been an SOS on the sand and that one 'plane at least had flown over the area in a period of perhaps only two years. Surely, in the intervening years – nearly five by my reckoning – another 'plane would fly close by the place. If the castaway had placed his letters well above the tide, and he was sensible enough to do that, of course, there seems to be no reason why they should not still be there, perhaps slightly covered by wind-blown sand but, on white sand, still very visible from the air. Well, as luck would have it, that may have been exactly what occurred.

The story I am about to tell you is simple enough, but it has reached me through several mouths and I do warn you that not only are sailors given to exaggeration, they are also given to fabrication. So you must take this tale as you see fit. It appears that a certain pilot, whose activities really don't bear investigation, flew over an island, one of an uninhabited group, in 1975, and saw an SOS on the beach. Intrigued, he noted its position on his charts and continued on his way. Now he is certainly a vagabond, this fellow, and probably a blackguard, too, but he isn't totally without heart. According to the story I received, he hastened with all speed to acquire a boat. Now, if it's the fellow I suspect it is, he owns more than one boat of his own. Be that as it may, he returned to the island and found it deserted.

Well, that's all there is, I'm afraid. Its location is still a mystery, but I'm pretty sure I could do something about that. I believe it's very close to where we finally ceased our search. I understand there is still a construction of stones there corresponding to your man's hut. The SOS, although not complete, remains untouched, and the trees are laden with coconuts. There was no skeleton. If you

173

feel inclined to indulge in another charter, I am sure I could accommodate you. So, if you can afford it and find this seaman's story sufficiently intriguing, please advise me at your convenience and I shall attempt to pinpoint the spot more accurately before spending your money.

Yours sincerely,

D. Hartley

I want to go. I badly want to go. But for what purpose? We know the trees are still there. We know that he is no longer there. Would any purpose be served by establishing beyond all doubt the exact location of the island? What would I gain in my knowledge of the castaway by walking over that barren spot, by touching his trees, by swimming over his reefs? What would I feel by touching those stones that he so laboriously piled up for his shelter? I would feel only sadness. And it would be a very expensive indulgence.

But I badly want to go.

THE END